VOICES

BY THE SAME AUTHOR

Wydddershyns
Unexpected Life Stories

Mrs Khan and the W.I. Bucket List

For children
(Writing as Dayzee Chayne)

The Robin Who Lost His song

Tintom and the Stripey Jumper

VOICES

'Those who wish to sing can
always find a song'
Swedish Proverb

by
Polly J. Fry

Illustrated
by
Barry Écuyer

Published by RHR
8 Brancepeth Place, Buckhurst Hill, Essex IG9 5JL

First published 2022
Copyright © Polly J. Fry

The moral right of Polly J. Fry to be identified as the author has been asserted in accordance with the Copyright, Designs and Patents Act of 1988

All rights reserved. No part of this publication may be reproduced, stored in a retrieval system, or transmitted in any form or by any means, electronic, mechanical, photocopied, recorded or otherwise without the permission of the copyright owner.

www.pollyjfrywriter
pollyjfrywriter@gmail.com

Internal design by Design for Writers

To PETER FRY
born when Capella (in Auriga)
was directly overhead,
although he didn't notice
it at the time.

CONTENTS

INTRODUCTION	*3*
WHAT IS A VOICE?	*3*
PART ONE: LOSING IT	*13*
GRANNIE LOUIE'S BIG ADVENTURE	
1 Grannie Louie Hitches A Lift	*22*
1965	*26*
The Lord Chancellor's Wife	*32*
The Sparkford Buddha	*37*
The Bay	*41*
Hugging Rabbits	*45*
Shall We Talk?	*59*
Teaching Mandarin	*68*
Consultations	
1 The Man	*74*
GRANNIE LOUIE'S BIG ADVENTURE	*84*
2 The UDD	*84*

PART 2: THE WILDERNESS YEARS   *91*

Grannie Louie's Big Adventure
-    3   Jake   *103*

Consultations
-    2   The Woman   *108*

The Van
-    1   The Woman   *116*

A Box Of Masks   *121*

The Van   *123*
-    2   The Neighbour   *123*

Freya's Outrage   *128*

The Van   *130*
-    3   The Man   *130*

Definitely Not Bunthorne's Bride   *134*

2015   *138*

Jessica   *151*

Dr Brock   *161*

The Podcast   *166*

The Soothsayer's Tale   *172*

The Lime Tree And The Gardener   *178*

Banger And The Poodle   *181*

Grannie Louie's Big Adventure
-    4   Time To Say Goodbye   *187*

FINALE: THE REBUILD   *193*

SWANSONG   *207*
USEFUL CONTACTS   *211*
ACKNOWLEDGEMENTS   *213*

AUTHOR'S NOTE

During the preparation of this book, Sue Ecuyer, Barry's wife, was taken seriously ill and sadly, subsequently died.

I'd like to thank Flo Sarlat for producing a frontispiece for us, albeit in a very different style. This does, however, fit in with the general theme of the book, which is the wide range of ways in which we communicate with one another.

Barry and I have done a lot together – and hopefully will again in the future – and although I didn't know Sue well, she was a lovely woman and I'm pleased to have met her on the occasions I did. She was a very talented craftswoman and those works she left are a tangible reminder of her presence.

Those of us who know Barry and knew Sue wish the whole family well

INTRODUCTION

WHAT IS A VOICE?

We all have a voice. Of course, not everyone's is audible to the human ear. Some are expressed through sign language; in another sense of the word, still others are expressed through writing, painting, dancing and movement or through a combination of all these things. However, they are not the nature of voice being addressed here, which is vocalised and carried on sound waves.

Our voices contain everything we've ever experienced, desired or feared. They reveal who we are physically, how we perceive ourselves and others, how we feel, our chronological age, what motivation lies behind our speech – I do mean everything. There is even evidence now that the voice can indicate physical illnesses such as diabetes and heart disease to those who know how to listen. It is a primary and largely unconscious element in how we relate to the world. A voice is not something to take for granted, although we all do.

It should be clear, then, that each individual's voice is a central aspect of his or her identity. Speaking to a friend recently, she told me that 'life is difficult enough when you lose your voice for a few days because of a cold. You feel somehow diminished'. In spite of being a 'serious' voice user, this had not been something I had thought of before but of course, it's absolutely true. This provides an insight

INTRODUCTION

into my own lack of insight, being, as I was, tied up in the loss of my own singing voice. It was I who had spent long, long hours trying to research the psychological impact of voice loss on singers and, surprisingly, that of regaining it, so missing something as fundamental as that wasn't very clever!

There are many definitions of the voice covering many different aspects of usage, and they can't all be fully explored here. At its simplest, 'a voice is the sound produced by humans and other vertebrates using the lungs and the vocal folds in the larynx, or voice box' (taken from the cover page of the National Institute on Deafness and Other Disorders, USA, found on the Internet). Voice is not necessarily vocalised as speech, however. Mammals mew, bark, howl, growl, cry, laugh and so on; birds sing. Babies produce gobbledegook and coo and I'm sure we've all heard of – even if we're not personally familiar with – the concept of billing and cooing and whispering sweet nothings. Again, these are not the aspects of voice I will be addressing in my narrative.

Vocalisation is generated by the passage of air from the lungs through the vocal folds, causing them to move closer together. If the airflow is under enough pressure, the folds – or cords, as they are more familiarly known – will vibrate. If for some reason the folds don't vibrate, speech is produced as a whisper. Each person's voice is as unique as his or her fingerprint. As intimated above, it helps define your personality; and as stated above, gives an indication of mood and health.

From this, it should be clear that the motive force for the voice is the breath, which we need also to sustain life, being the vehicle (as it is) for the exchange of carbon dioxide – a waste product – and oxygen, essential for survival.

WHAT IS A VOICE?

This is all so much part of the everyday life of most human doings, we're not even conscious of it unless it fails us.

When I 'lost' my ability to sing, I lost everything. This is not hyperbole stemming from an inflated ego but a statement of fact. My world fell apart and my sense of self with it. For a singer, it is the identity, reason for living, the element within you conferring self-esteem and the much deeper self-worth; that aspect of you that makes you most happy, most frustrated, that gives most satisfaction and makes you despair when you can't make it work the way you want it to. Of course, there will be other things in life that are extremely important but mostly these are not part of our anatomy and not usually part of how we relate to the wider world at a fundamental level.

Voice loss is very personal. Those people I've spoken to who have experienced it don't want to be named and I understand that. Whilst the impact is, in some respects, universal, in others it is particular to the individual and too intimate to talk about.

Voice loss was described by one singer thus:

> **It wasn't just a question of having missed out on years of performing, it was the loss of all that self-esteem. Everything goes, your identity, your sense of self.**

Another expressed her experience as follows:

> **One of the greatest blows was that I could no longer sing. It's tempting to glibly write, 'Not that singing played a huge part in my life...' but that wouldn't be true. It may not be my**

INTRODUCTION

profession or my ambition, but singing has sustained me for as long as I can remember.

She states later

It was like losing a part of my soul

Yet another, a friend and talented amateur singer, told me,

The whole of life shrank. There was a shadow over eveything I did, even the shopping

It's clear, then, that losing a voice isn't the same as breaking a finger nail.

I think we can safely say there has been a renaissance regarding the importance of singing, and that such as Gareth Malone have made it once again 'cool' to sing. There are loads of choirs around now, from community choirs to dementia choirs and singing for recreation has, again, taken the place it deserves.

When I was singing for a living, I was frequently told 'Well, I do that too, but I do it after a day's work.' Or 'You do take it all seriously, don't you. It's only singing and we can all do that.' Whilst I agree that we can all sing, we don't all spend years being trained vocally and musically so that we can do it well and stand in front of a paying audience doing so.

It's undoubtedly the case that there is a lot more understanding and 'sympathy' now than when my own voice failed, but at that time, I was told things such as 'It's no big deal. Do something else.' 'What's all the fuss about? I've never been able to sing.' 'Why are you making such a song and dance about it? It's not as if you can't do other things.' – among other very (un)helpful comments.

WHAT IS A VOICE?

I accept that these people probably thought they were being supportive but the fact remains that they weren't. I asked one of them how they would respond if a footballer had an injury and was no longer able to play and was informed 'That's different. Football's a skill. You have to work at it, hone it. Anyone can sing.' The whole point was that I couldn't (in spite of having worked at it, honed it) but this response does reflect the attitude of society towards singing at that time – or at least, the society with which I was acquainted.

The vocal apparatus is robust, far more robust than we, as singers, give it credit for. But, if abused, it will pay you back in kind.

Of course, not all singers will have quite such a dramatic or all-encompassing response to the loss of a voice, but then, not that many singers lose their voices so totally as I did (or maybe, not many singers admit to it) and if they do have problems, in my experience they are unwilling to talk about it. Singers who are still 'intact' don't want to talk about it either, almost as if they do, it might happen to them as well. It hadn't occurred to me before this happened that voice loss could actually be a taboo subject, but there we are.

Women are much more prone to voice difficulties than men, probably the most significant being those due to the changes experienced during the course of the monthly cycle. This is one of the challenges we have to learn to overcome in the course of training. Pregnancy and post-partum is another 'danger time', when it isn't that uncommon to lose the voice altogether, although mostly it will return. This is in addition to all the everyday occurrences that can impact the voice. This does not mean that men don't have their problems, simply that they are likely to have different origins, physical and psychological alike.

The voice is tied up with our emotions and expresses them whether we intend it to or not. I have no doubt that

INTRODUCTION

this can be, and is, a contributor to men's – as well as women's – vocal difficulties when they arise and could, at times, be the primary cause. I'm not qualified to judge.

Add to this the everyday challenges of dust, pollen, heat, cold, rising noise levels – to say nothing of physical illness and discomfort. There are many booby traps out there for the professional voice user to negotiate.

I always maintained that whilst the initial loss of my own voice was physical, not getting it back was psychological. I still believe that to be true and that is, without a doubt, the obstacle to reinstating what I would consider to be a 'usable' instrument.

A friend, an accomplished singer who has sung all her life in an amateur choir, told me that voice loss is commonplace and most singers suffer at some point or other. I don't doubt this is an accurate observation, but I couldn't find any willing to discuss it with me, so I had no way of knowing if my experiences were *de rigeur* or me being melodramatic, which was the response of non-singing friends, acquaintances and others, as we've seen above. Research is now being done at City University, London, by speech therapist Aparna Ramachandran, herself a singer who once had voice difficulties (thankfully now resolved), who is looking at how individuals work with the instrument to overcome their problems. I am extremely pleased to know that this work is being done. My own interest is in what it does to us psychologically, whether we get it back or not, but obviously, the physical and psychological can't be totally separate.

My own 'journey' (as we now have to name such things) has been tough – far tougher than I would ever have imagined – and even more surprising, it remains so, even though I can sing again after a fashion.

WHAT IS A VOICE?

Everything I have said above can be expressed far more succinctly by quoting the online information for the British Voice Association's 2022 conference:

> **Your voice is entirely unique. Your acoustic profile identifies, even verifies you. Intriguingly, your voice reveals: who you are, how you feel, where you've been, and who and what you've been listening to. Those who work professionally with voices, scientist or artist, know that a voice is more than distinctive acoustic or physiology. A voice is personal: formed by mind, language and culture, and central to a concept of self.**

The conference was called, quite simply 'I am my voice'.

*

The following narrative goes through the process of voice loss and the slow process of acceptance – *Losing It*; adjustment, also looking at the possible different influences on the physical processes and the establishing of life in the absence of song – *The Wilderness Years* ; and then enters the difficult period of learning to sing again – *The Rebuild*. These sections, as in my earlier *Wyddershyns* are separated by short stories. It isn't an academic paper and lacks the rigour required for one – indeed, it lacks any rigour at all – but a purely personal account of my experience, in the hope that someone out there might benefit from it; and who knows, someone might even pick up the topic

INTRODUCTION

as a focus for research, although given research is a costly business and there are so many causes chasing so few resources, it's unlikely to happen.

Although the quotes are real, they are not attributed to the person making them for the reason stated above: I haven't had their permission to identify them.

Hopefully, you will enjoy the stories separating the sections of narrative, some of them if not all. This isn't a misery memoir and the point of writing is for entertainment as well as to 'inform'. Thank you in advance for reading this account of my own difficulties. I hope you never find the same thing happens to you.

The human voice is the most perfect instrument of all

Arvo Part

PART ONE

LOSING IT

I'm not going into details about how it happened. Suffice it to say it was entirely my own fault for doing something incredibly stupid that I knew I shouldn't be doing.

A sudden, sharp pain travelled across the front of my throat on the right hand side. My voice cut out immediately and it was impossible to carry on singing. The sensation was extremely unpleasant and even speaking caused discomfort with a change in the timbre of my voice. Even *attempting* to sing hurt my throat too much to continue and resulted in pain up the inside of my neck/throat to the part of my ear behind the drum, as well as the obvious places.

I think I should explain that I have no real interest in the past, whether it be in the form of history as presented by text books and popular TV programmes; or my own former life (-ves). I say 'lives' because I've been lucky enough to have packed rather more in than many people have the chance to manage.

For me, once something is over, it's over. Its value will be processed subconsciously and doesn't require any intervention from me. It's a bit more difficult with the happiest moments. It's fun to rehearse them over and over again; but time spent doing that is time not fully experienced in the now, so not a great idea. As far as the unpleasant events are concerned – well, they can't be relived and put right, so what's the point? There are times when this isn't as easy as I would like it to be, but it's the right way for me. There are, of course, occasions when memories can be beneficial and as I have a good powers of recall, this can be put to good use.

One of the things I decided when young was that given we only get one opportunity to experience the world, I was going to follow every single break presented to me. It was a good decision. Among other things, it means that whatever mistakes I've made have been entirely of my own creation and there's no-one to blame. But, these factors combined mean that whilst I can guarantee that the facts of this narrative are accurate, the same isn't necessarily true for the details of emotional memory, which is notoriously difficult to pin down even at the best of times. However, what I can be sure of is that voice loss was devastating and the realisation of that was slow in its evolution.

My initial reaction was that it was an almighty inconvenience but if I rested the instrument for a few days, it would sort itself out. It didn't. I waited a month and contacted BAPAM [the contact details for this, and other relevant organisations, are listed at the end of the book]. This is an excellent body working with the medical problems experienced by performing artists, who suggested an ENT person to me who had specialist knowledge of the 'voice user's throat'.

He did a pretty extensive examination and told me he could see nothing seriously wrong, that I should rest it and it would come back. Reassured, I decided to be patient. Whilst this is easy enough in general, it wasn't so straightforward in relation to my voice. It was still uncomfortable at times to speak – less so and not as frequent – but as far as I could tell, being able to sing again was no closer.

Having grown up surrounded by poverty and unemployment, my working life can be characterised as what is now known as a portfolio career, although I did dip in and out of mental health over the years in a variety of capacities. In those days, not following a single strand, striving to move up and up via promotion on a specific career trajectory – or even wanting to – was frowned on as 'not knowing what I wanted' and being flippant and flighty. Nothing could have been further from the truth. I knew exactly what I wanted. It was a case of not being prepared to get it in ways that seemed to me inefficient at best and unmanageable at worst; also, I didn't want to channel everything into one activity only to find it didn't work and I ended up broke. However much criticism I was obliged to withstand for my choice of lifestyle, it stood me in good stead in this instance – and has continued to do so – as it meant that there were other sources of income and I could keep a roof over my head and pay the bills.

At this point, I maintained contact with my musician friends and professional contacts, assuming that we would be working together again in the not-too-distant future.

The world of classical music is small and closely knit. Moreover, like any professional corpus whatever that may be, a shared history is created in the form of a more-or-less common training and a communal present, where you're all in it together and understand first-hand the pressures and joys of your chosen career. You have an instinctive understanding of other musicians. This is true even if you don't much like them. At those times when you're playing/singing and even when you're not to a greater or lesser degree, you're a unit. That is a valuable commodity, too precious to lose or relinquish without a fight. In any case, why should I have done so? I believed my situation was temporary.

As time went on and nothing was changing, I got increasingly concerned, returned to the original ENT guy, who said the same thing as before, although he did suggest physiotherapy and ordered some physical tests, the nature of which I can't remember. Friends were asking about my singing and I was having to explain to them, musicians and non-musicians alike, that for the time being, I was unable to sing. No-one among the non-musicians was particularly sympathetic, which in itself didn't matter much. What did matter, though, was the idea frequently presented to me that 'it was only singing'. I could still speak and that's what mattered. That I could concentrate now on 'a proper job' and – as far as my family were concerned – get the career that I should have been pursuing all along. When pressed, none of them could give me any indication as to what this might be, but there were very definitely many more respectable and worthy ways of making a living than using my voice, which was, after all, something that they did *as well as* working for a living. It didn't matter that they didn't understand; but that they weren't willing to accept my point of view was as valid as theirs and that my distress was self-indulgence did bother me.

After about six months, having tried homoeopathy, naturopathy, acupuncture and meditation, I decided to try a different tack and asked my GP to refer me to a local ENT specialist. The GP was extremely understanding and got me an appointment within a couple of weeks. Such things were possible in those days. I won't relate the details here beyond telling you that the throat man sprayed the back of my mouth with anaesthetic, something for which I have still not forgiven him, and after doing all he had to do, said there was nothing he could find wrong.

When it got to a year, I realised that my singing career was over and it was quite possible that I would never sing again even for fun around the house. It was like having my soul ripped out.

***

The rest of life carried on as normal. I still did the other work I was being paid to do, had family responsibilities and a good-enough social life, continuing to live in as familiar a fashion as I could. However, I couldn't bear being on the outside looking in, so cut myself from all the musicians in my circle, stopped learning new music and listening to the radio, ignored my extensive collection of sheet music and CDs. The piano did nothing but gather dust and I started the process of trying to reinvent myself without music.

As I'd come to singing more or less accidentally, somewhere in the back of my mind I must have believed that something else would come along to which I would feel equally committed and with which I would have as strong an identification. I was walking round a lake in the local park one afternoon when I realised that this, too, was not going to happen. It felt as if I'd been kicked in the gut.

The period of adjustment was difficult and slow, although probably quicker than I remember it being. Again, apart from the underlying awareness that there was something fundamental missing, what I found really hard was the attitude of other people, who regarded it as no big deal and couldn't – or wouldn't – understand what the issue was. This is a point I won't labour, as I've made it above and providing more of their comments and observations isn't going to illuminate things any further. But, I felt totally isolated, alone with a problem no-one could understand or even more significantly, had no interest in trying to. If I brought the subject up, there were either glazed eyes or 'not this again' or – even worse 'get a life'. No-one was willing to talk over with me the fact that for me, at that time, it felt as if my life was over. Indeed, life as I knew it definitely was.

There are only two times in my time that I've felt lonely and I hope this was the last. I also felt let down, as I'd made

LOSING IT

a point of always being available for anyone wanting an ear, no matter how trivial I felt their difficulties to be – and we all think at times that the problems people present to us are insignificant, however hard we try not to – but there was no-one willing to offer me the same support.

For a long time, my days were lived on automatic pilot. This itself was a strange phenomenon, as whatever I'd done – and there was a lot of it – I gave myself to it heart and soul. But at that point, everything had lost its shine and although I did some wonderful things, they really didn't do much for me and there was little satisfaction from them. This (if you believe those around me and you're perfectly entitled to) was because I was a prima donna and attention seeker. However, I lost everything in that silly moment when I acted on a foolish whim and had no idea how to start reinstating myself in a new image.

**

The turning point came when I joined the local Wildlife Trust. The natural world had always been of great interest to me and now I had more time, I decided to explore whatever was local. I lived on the edge of a forest – the largest area of ancient woodland in Britain, so I learned – in a county with everything but mountains. At university, I'd been drawn towards marine biology, particularly the seashore and salt marshes, so there was the germ of an interest already there in me to try to grow.

I'd found a lifeline.

I cannot imagine a more satisfying calling than my own: beauty, humanity, and history every day, combined with the cathartic joy of singing

Renee Fleming

GRANNIE LOUIE'S BIG ADVENTURE

Part 1: Grannie Louie Hitches A Lift

'Granny Louie's lost some marbles, mum.' Jake threw his jacket on the sofa, in spite of being told at least a thousand times that he should hang it on the coat stand; and made his way to the kitchen to raid the fridge.

'What's she done now?' asked his mother, a weary tone suffusing every vowel and consonant. She had more than enough to do without sorting out Mrs Robertson Snr.

Grannie Louie, however, far from losing anything, was probably the only one of them genuinely on the ball when it came to the Strange Goings On at *The Earl of Southampton*. She'd decided a long time ago she didn't want to be one of these 'modern' grannies, just as likely to be found jumping out of a light aircraft or trekking through the Himalayas as snuggling down in the evening with a cocoa and a bit of chick-lit for the over-sixties. She wanted to be someone like her own grandmother had been – cosy, welcoming and easy going, a place of refuge if the grandchildren needed one. She'd never bothered to colour her hair, hadn't updated her wardrobe, rarely wore make-up and had made a point of not getting a mobile phone. It wasn't that she didn't want one or that it wouldn't make her life easier. It definitely would; but it would be a nod to the twenty first century and she'd rather enjoyed the twentieth.

PART 1: GRANNIE LOUIE HITCHES A LIFT

Her group of friends went regularly to the *Earl* for a pensioner's lunch and sometimes Josie and Rick took her there for a Sunday roast. Grannie Louie had been noticing all those strange people with the pointy ears and pudding basin haircuts. Their eyes were such an odd colour and the pupils were more like you see in a cat than a human. Her friends couldn't see what she was driving at and the family couldn't be bothered to try. 'Men from Mars, indeed,' said Rick Robertson. 'My mother's bonkers.'

Grannie Louie was only seventy three, nothing these days; and rather resented the idea that she could be judged as infirm, when it was totally clear that these people were Not Normal. Naturally, she knew that nobody could define normal. When she was a physiotherapist, they'd said over and over again 'We can't say what normal is but we all recognise when something isn't.' It'd been a sound way of looking at things but these days 'Normal is the new Not-Normal' she'd decided, and there were a lot of people who agreed with her.

***

'HI there,' said one of the Not-Normal people, intercepting Grannie Louie on the way back to the table after visiting the Little Girls' Room ('How twee can you get,' she thought.' We all have to use them.') 'We see you here a lot. Is it a favourite haunt?

Should she answer? Josie and Rick were convinced she was going doolally already. If she started talking to these guys, who they claimed not to be able to see, what would they think then? She glanced around and there was no-one observing her, so she took a chance. 'It's been a meeting place for years. They look after us well.'

'Do you ever meet up elsewhere?'

She was a bit more cautious about answering this. Say they wanted to abduct her and subject her to all sorts of unspeakable tests? You read about them sometimes in the paper. He looked okay but then, that's surely how these people got their way. Sensing her disquiet, he continued 'Look, please don't feel pressured. I'll give you my card and if you'd like to meet again, give me a ring.'

Wow! Thought Grannie Louie. I'm being picked up! At my age! None of the crowd will believe me! And then she realised, no, they wouldn't. They couldn't even see that these folk were different. 'It's all in her mind,' they kept saying. 'She's imagining it all.' If she told them now that one of them had approached her and asked her on a date – well, maybe not a date exactly, but you can see what she meant – they'd undoubtedly get the doctor out like she'd overheard them saying they would. 'No time like the present,' she thought. 'I don't want your card. Let's go somewhere and chat.'

In the blink of an eye and who-knows-how, she found herself in a very attractive homestead, a bit like an upmarket mobile home (static home, really) with a computer console at one end and all mod cons at the other. He showed her round, chatted with her, asked her all about herself – it was all above board and perfectly affable. No signs of laboratories. No remnants of previous visitors subjected to research never to be 'normal' again. No need to have worried, to be fair. In the blink of another eye and who-knows-how, she found herself back at the table where she'd left her friends. Boy, she had so much to tell them! But they just looked at her like she'd had some sort of brainstorm and carried on talking, even Pat, who was off at the weekend for an Adults Ballet Course and Barbara, doing something frightfully

PART 1: GRANNIE LOUIE HITCHES A LIFT

clever with the poems of Gerard Manley Hopkins. They did notice, though, that her face was smoother and there were flecks of brown in amongst the grey; and over the coming weeks, during their cherished First Fifteen Minutes, when they were all allowed to moan about their aches and pains, Grannie Louie didn't join in anymore.

She regularly met 167, whose name she later discovered to be Kaydock; and he explained that they were here on holiday and didn't talk about things like age, because time is an academic construct that they had little interest in. At one time, she'd have been mystified, but now, she knew exactly what they meant.

Back in her granny flat, Rick and Josie had noticed that instead of the romances and books about retirees suddenly discovering they had a talent for neurosurgery or intercontinental exploration, she was reading science books. Real science, the hard core stuff. Not science fiction but text books and Learned Journals; and she wasn't interested in joining them for dinner anymore. Too busy, she said, although for the life of them they couldn't see how.

'I've been talking to 167,' she revealed by mistake when they were haranguing her about the changes in her. 'He's been explaining to me how they manage to get me to their ship using thought travel,'

'I've had enough of this Rick,' Josie informed her long-suffering husband. 'I know she's your mother but enough is enough. She reckons they've invited her to go on interstellar travel with them. I'm definitely getting the doctor in.'

'Bugger that,' thought Grannie Louie, overhearing the conversation on returning from visiting her new friends. '167! Kaydock!' She projected her thoughts just like he'd taught her to. 'Get the spare room ready! I'm coming with you.'

Grannie Louie was never seen again.

1965

Laura wondered how much longer this could go on. She'd been stuck in here for weeks now, doing her very best to do everything required of her. She knew she was mad – they kept telling her, so it must be right. They kept reminding her 'the mad person can never see it. Mad people always think they're the sane ones and it's the rest of the world that's got the problem.' So, she'd just have to get used to it and do what was expected. Then it'd all be okay

It'd started when she lost interest in the cooking. 'What's so special about cooking anyway?' she asked herself. 'You spend all afternoon in the kitchen doing the preparations and in five minutes, it's all been eaten.' So she'd started to make sandwiches instead. Much better. It only took five minutes to make a sandwich. Not even that, really. But John hadn't been at all happy. 'It's what wives do,' he told her. 'A decent meal is the least a man can expect.'

'Why should he expect anything?' She posed the question to herself, knowing there was little point in extending it to the wider world. 'It wasn't my idea to give up my job and become a housewife. That was John.' He wasn't going to have any wife of his working, he'd informed her. 'How many wives is he intending to have?' she wondered but again, didn't bother to articulate it.

It was okay for John. He was out all day working. She didn't really know what it was he did. Too complicated, he'd explained, and as long as he brought the housekeeping home, she didn't need to know anything more than that he earned a decent wage. 'Decent enough, I suppose,' she decided. 'It buys the food and the bits for the regular upkeep of the house.' And she couldn't complain. He took her out on Saturdays sometimes, and every so often gave her some money to buy a new dress. She counted her blessings. At least she had a good home and the cupboards were always stocked.

But things got worse. She suggested that she should get a job. Not full-time, of course, just something to stop her getting bored.

'Bored?' he'd replied, with a puzzled expression. 'Bored? How can you be bored? You've got the house to keep clean, the dinner to prepare as well as your own lunch to make, all the shopping and the washing, ironing, washing up – what on earth are you complaining about? It's not as if we need the money.'

Well, put like that, she supposed he was right. But truly, it really did seem a bit mundane. It had been fun when she was out at work. She had all her friends in the company and the daily challenge of doing it well. It was different every day. Not major differences, of course. Being a receptionist was nothing very much, as he'd told her often. Anyone could do that and of course, he was right. He always was. But she had liked working a lot. There were a load of wide-ranging clients coming in and out and all had queries to be addressed, sometimes needing nothing more from her than a cup of tea and a comfortable seat while they were waiting to be seen but sometimes, she had to do all sorts of things to answer their queries, before they even got as far as their appointments. She liked that. Often they'd chat with her and tell her about their lives or their work. Her colleagues were interesting, too, and they'd laughed together and shared meals.

She missed them but it all had to change when she got married – well, women weren't expected to work, were they? It looked bad for the man, if his wife was out at work. It meant he couldn't support her and that wasn't right. She understood what he was saying but it really was extremely dull, being at home all day with no-one to talk to except the shopkeepers and there was never much conversation with them. She realised she was being unreasonable and ungrateful and he was right, she must buck up her ideas and adjust. That was it. Everyone said that being married was something you had to grow into and make the effort, so that's what she'd have to do. She'd try harder. And that's exactly what she did.

PART 1: GRANNIE LOUIE HITCHES A LIFT

It was okay for a bit. Everything was turned into a challenge. How clean could she get the curtains? Could she make the table shine just a little bit brighter? She did loads of research, went round all the different shops looking for the best products and tried them all out, only he told her she was spending too much money and not at all wisely. There were two different brands of things in the cupboards, sometimes three and it just wasn't necessary. It was a waste. He didn't go out to work every day to have his money thrown down the drain. That was a bit of surprise, because he'd always said it was their money, not just his, but maybe that was another idea she'd have to adjust to.

Then, sitting in the lounge watching him watching the television, she noticed they weren't going out as much as they used to. The TV was on in the afternoons on Saturdays now, sport and things, and he'd had a hard week at work and needed a bit of leisure time. His Saturday afternoons were spent enjoying the wrestling and football in the winter, cricket in the summer.

The months were passing, threatening to turn into years; and she wasn't adjusting at all. She was hating it all and the worst thing was when they went to bed and she felt him coming towards her and well, not exactly demanding his rights but certainly claiming them without any consultation with her.

***

'Divorce?' he queried. 'Are you mad?'

'Well, we don't really get on very well, do we?' she'd answered.

'What are you talking about?' he asked her.

'Well, we don't sit down and talk, or go out much, not even to the pub.'

1965

'I do a day's work, woman,' he'd said.

'Yes, but I'm stuck here every day and I get bored,' she told him.

'Not this again. How do you suppose you'll live?' he asked her.

'Well, I could get a job, like I had before we were married.'

He laughed. Told her she was being ridiculous and didn't know when she was well off. Did she think his life was so wonderful? Going off to the bank every day and having to do all the thinking for both of them, earning the money to pay for the house and yes, to pay for her too.

'But I'm just not happy,' she told him.

And that's how she'd ended up here.

They were teaching her how to be a proper woman and wife again. Encouraging her to cook, getting her involved with the cleaning on the ward, doing the washing up, making the beds, sewing – all the things that normal, sane women did and enjoyed. And they reminded her how lucky she was, having such a kind, hard-working husband. Sometimes she felt ashamed but others, well, others she just wondered what life was all about.

She'd seen lots of people wandering the corridors who'd been there years and didn't want to be like them, so she'd best knuckle down, prove she was sane enough to go home.

John came in to see her on Sunday afternoons. He didn't stop long and most of the time was spent talking to the people running the ward about how she was doing. She got the feeling she must be getting better, because she was much more willing to do the chores and complaining less, so surely she couldn't be as mad as she had been.

***

1965

And now she was back home and from absolutely nowhere came one of those sudden flashes of realisation. This was how it felt to be sane. She knew she was sane because since John had collected her a few weeks ago, she was doing everything she was supposed to do. She didn't even object when she felt his hand pulling up her nightie in the early hours of the morning; just screwed up her face – he couldn't see it through the darkness, so she knew it'd be okay – and put up with it until he was finished.

***

The house was spotless. The dinner was on the table. The cupboards were full with just the right amount of provisions.

Making the after-dinner tea that night, she thought: 'Everyone knows I'm mad. At least, I was mad once, and if you've been mad once, you're always mad, so I can't really be blamed for my actions, can I?'

She put the tea in the pot and poured the water on it. Then, she bent down to the cupboard under the sink and got the rat poison out.

That should do the trick.

THE LORD CHANCELLOR'S WIFE

Hello everyone. Most of you won't have heard of me. Not now. Years ago – well, maybe not that long ago really, fifty years or so? Like this morning to us in the fairy world. Okay, no matter – everyone would have heard of me back then. I'm Iolanthe, the fairy who married a mortal and was immortalised – if a fairy can be immortalised, given that we're immortal already – in the eponymous operetta by G and S. Definitely their best. Oh yes. No doubt about that. They were on fire when they wrote about me. Maybe that's where they got the inspiration for the song the Fairy Queen sings to the Head of the Fire Service. Now there's a thought.

Anyway, as you most likely won't have heard of me, I'd better fill you in a bit. I got banished to the bottom of a horrible, slimy pond because I married the Lord Chancellor. Golly gee, he was a handsome lad! I only fancied a change from the fairy men, really, only it got a bit out of hand and I found myself in the family way. Not that there's anything wrong with the fairies, you understand. They're really nice. Especially Cobweb. That Robin Goodfellow's a bit of a pest, though. Always playing what he calls pranks but they're really a silly nuisance, like when he poured honey all over my dandelion leaf, so when I tried to get up I got stuck to it and had to take my dress off before I could fly away. It was one of my nicest, too. He thought it was a hoot but then, he's only young, about three hundred and sixty four, so he has time to learn. And he's the exception.

It's just that when this Human came along, it seemed like it might be an idea to try something different. I mean, immortality means you're around for a long time. You don't know what you're missing if you don't try it and honestly, he really was dazzling. And so kind and caring. No honey pots near any chairs in his vicinity. Not even at breakfast, I discovered after the nuptials. Anyway, we had a boy, Strephon we called him, big strapping lad who fell in love with Phyllis. Only once I'd been banished to be pestered by dragon fly larvae and the like, the LC fell in love with Phyllis too. Well, I wasn't having that! My boy's happiness at stake because of my husband? Give me a break. No chance whatsoever. Strephon's half man and half fairy, by the way. A fairy down to the waist and a bloke further down. Or maybe the other way round. Immaterial, really, he sort of exists in no-one's land, as it were, with no-one wanting to claim him for their own. Anyway, to get to the point, by the end of the opera, the LC knows I'm his long lost wife (who he thought had kicked the bucket) Strephon gets it on with Phyllis and all the fairies are married to Peers of the Realm, except the Fairy Queen, who cops off with Private Willis. Not sure why she didn't end up with the fireman. She makes such a moving appeal to him but maybe he was busy putting fires out elsewhere. Besides, he only appears in song so as the Private couldn't be left unattached, it made sense to get the two of them together. Hmm. A Fairy Queen and a Private. Recipe for disaster? Only time will tell.

Anyway, it's all supposed to be hunky dory because we've all ended up in nice pairs with rings on our fingers, and that's where the opera ends, with lovely music and great fun and games being had by all. It's a really good opera, if you're interested. Give it a go yourselves, if you

THE LORD CHANCELLOR'S WIFE

don't believe me. Anyway, folks, let me tell you. Life isn't necessarily that straightforward.

For a start, you're miles bigger than we are, so we had to use our special magic to get up to your size and that alone is exhausting. But good grief! You can't imagine how cumbersome one of your big, lumbering bodies is! Although perhaps you can. I'm assuming if you're reading this, you're a Human yourself. You might be a fairy, of course. But truly, the strain on knees and hips from having to support all that weight and your feet ache practically all the time. Awful, especially as you lot don't fly at all, not even a short distance, but walk on pavements and bridges and things. I had a corn!!! Yes, I really, honestly did! A corn! Me, who survived life at the bottom of a pond with frogs and someone's coy carp trying to eat me all the time. The indignity of it! Fairy feet aren't meant to be encased in shoes. Well, I guess that's what comes from liaisons with a mortal. It might be why we're forbidden to marry them. I'll have to ask.

The next thing, of course, is that the LC didn't want to do exciting things like going for an awayday along the river bank or talk about soothing things like the wild thyme and eglantine. Oh no. He wanted to talk about The Law. Specifically, his boring court cases. He told me once about a woman sooing someone or other (I never did find out what sooing is) because she had a snail in her ginger beer. He wasn't a bit upset about the poor snail in that most disgusting of human beverages but was really exercised about how dreadful it was for a woman to find a snail. What a total wimp! They're sweet things when you make the effort to get to know them. I tried to put him right but of course, he's the LC, so he knew best.

Then there's the washing and ironing. You'd think with all the money the LC earns, he'd have everything laundered but oh no. That was down to Yours Truly. And those clothes are so dreadfully scratchy. I got rips all over my lovely, delicate wings and my poor hands grew as rough as a slug's tongue. Not that I used my wings much, of course, because they couldn't support those horrible unwieldy frames. They're a bit like butterfly wings, really, and you know how fragile they are. Pity I didn't fall in love with a butterfly. They don't last very long so if it didn't work out, it wouldn't matter much. And the food! OMG. The food. If you don't mind, I don't even want to think about it.

And, of course, it almost goes without saying that there was no more gazing into my eyes and telling me how beautiful I am. It was all 'you go up, dear. I'll join you later.' Not much fun in that, let me tell you.

Anyway, because it was me who started the trend that meant all the fairy women had to marry a mortal, it was me who got the blame. Imagine! After the way they'd all admired them and venerated them, and so I said to the Fairy Queen, 'Okay, if that's how you feel, banish me to another slimy pond.' So she did and that's how I've ended up here. Sitting on a rock watching the sticklebacks and pond snails. I've warned them to steer clear of ginger beer cans, of course.

THE SPARKFORD BUDDHA

Okay. Here we go again. Two hours if there are no problems on the roads. Most of it's quite pleasant, so no reason to complain. Not really. Maybe it's the contempt bred of familiarity. Every single metre of this road has been travelled a million times, all of them by me. Maybe a different route would be in order? Note to self: consider it for next time.

Landmark One. The Bottleneck at Lyndhurst. I really will take the time (at some point) to have a look round, see if there's anything interesting here. A charity shop maybe, or something quirky and unusual. From my strategic position here in the queue for the lights, all I can see are a bakery and a haberdasher's. Not many of them around anymore. I wonder if they do good business? Whoops, being barked at by the driver behind, the light must have gone green. Off we go again.

I keep meaning to time it so that I can try out that Thai place on the way. Joe says it's really good and he's pretty reliable. Pity they don't do cookery classes. Mind you, where would you get the right ingredients for preparing the stuff at home? Do you suppose they'd sell them to the people they teach? Hypothetical, of course. They don't do lessons. *Through the Looking Glass*. Lessons. A misnomer because the knowledge they confer increases rather than diminishing. I guess logically they should be called morons, but it doesn't give quite the right impression.

Now, this is the sort of hold up I really don't mind. Sheep on the road. Loads of them. I'd happily sit here and watch them all day but that woman over the other side doesn't look particularly happy. She's keeps gesticulating at me. What does she expect me to do? Charm them with my winning personality and lovely smile? Or maybe she thinks I'm like the Pied Piper and have a flute in the back to lure them away with. Whatever I can do she can too, so I think I'll just sit tight and see what transpires. Ah. Here she goes. Storming around stamping at them. True, they're scattering but they'll be back. Gosh, she must be driving through at about eighty mph. Should I have warned her about the mobile speed camera? Too late now.

Trees, donkeys, sunshine spilling through onto the tarmac. It's a pleasure to be on the road.

Landmark Two: The Spire of Salisbury Cathedral, heralding the approach to the Ring Road Bottleneck. At least the weather's on my side. Yay! Last time it was unbearably hot even with the air conditioning up as high as it would go. Is that why those tuk-tuk thingies have no sides? Joe says they're being sold over here now. Not the most comfortable form of transport so I'm told, but we should always make up our own minds based on evidence, not hearsay, so I won't take his word for it.

My visits west have seen me through every imaginable calamity as well as the discovery of many wonderful things I could never even have hoped for – friends, experiences, places, even that funny little shrub with the gorgeous jewel – like flowers and the horrible aroma. There are no bad associations at all. My bolthole. But more than that. My spiritual home? Who can say. We never know where something might lead. It certainly wasn't planned as anything more than a single trip for birdwatching and became the mainstay of my existence. I wonder if my St Francis is still on that altar in Glastonbury? If I ask them again to sell him to me, they'll probably have me prosecuted for harassment, so maybe stick to admiring it. And there's the baker's, of course. No trip to Somerset is ever complete without the full range of baked goodies. Are they calorie free? I never put any weight on, in spite of the vast volume consumed.

Watch the speedometer. Miles of road ahead with no external stimuli. Easy to get carried away. Concentrate. On what?

***

Nothing on the radio. What do people think when they see you shouting into the ether? Do they realise you're telling the radio how to behave or talking on the mobile phone, or do they think you're having a conversation with yourself? Lots of good reasons for doing that, according to my news feed, apart from the obvious ones.

I'm glad we never came here together. There'd be bound to be memories to create a lump in the throat. Is he okay? Of course he is.

Good. The last turn off until we go right towards the 372. Another twenty miles or so.

Joe. Probably the most significant relationship I ever had. Is that because it was the most enigmatic? What on earth were we thinking? Perhaps we weren't thinking at all. There are those who say we should listen to our hearts and ignore our heads and it probably works for them. Never did much for me though. Where is he now? Does he let me live rent free in his head the way I let him occupy mine? I hope not. Enough that one of us is battered and confused.

About halfway along this stretch of the road now. Lord, it's boring. Shall I play I Spy?

***

THE SPARKFORD BUDDHA

There's something strange about the way we hold on to pain, like it validates our experience, makes it worth something. Or am I being cynical? Could be that it protects us against letting it happen again. Except we always do. We always convince ourselves this time it's different, but it never is of course. We want to believe there's a pot of gold at the end of the rainbow. Or a happy-ever-after, at the very least. Why did no-one ever tell us it's the happy-in-this-moment that counts? If we sort that out, the happy-ever-after takes care of itself. And we can't find it outside ourselves. It happens within. Blimey, where did all that come from?

Ah, here we go. Any minute now. Yep, just the few last trees. Wait for it.....

The Sparkford Buddha! Serene and radiant, keeping watch over the road. This is the start of My Somerset. Lovely to see you again.

Turn right. Yep. It's good to be home.

THE BAY

'That's the woman from up the road. The millionaire recluse. The one wot keeps a pet unicorn.'

'Right. Yes. Erm….. Well, how do you know it's her then, if she's a recluse?' Adele was used to this kind of encounter. It was the sort of place that attracted eccentrics. It was the same in all seaside towns. She'd observed it often but could never understand why.

'You can tell by that great mane of hair. Just like her pet. They says if she's seen walking out, it don't bode right. Bad things will occur.'

'Right,' replied Adele. 'Well, thank you for your time. You've been most helpful.'

She went back to the car. He'd been pleasant enough, even offered her a cup of tea and a biscuit but she really didn't think she'd enjoy either one of them standing out on the doorstep in the pouring rain for the best part of an hour, so she politely declined.

'Damn,' she said. 'Soaked through to the bone.' She drove up to the bay just in time to get into the little café, where she treated herself to a filter coffee and a cheese sandwich. She could afford neither but what the hell? It wasn't often she indulged herself.

She quite liked doing this market research. It could be fitted in round her acting jobs – fewer than there used to be – and she met lots of really nice people. Even the eccentric ones were good to spend time with, often more interesting than the others. Some of the surveys were really fascinating, like the transport survey and the one on health perception. Who would have imagined there'd be so much to it? She had three more interviews before she finished for the day. It was going to be a late-ish night by the time she got through them all. Still, she was used to late nights. In her 'real' job, she sometimes worked right through the night and in the theatre, she never got home before the early hours.

The sun was setting over the bay and now the rain had stopped, she paused a while looking out over the sea, watching the great orb of light slowing sinking into the horizon. It wasn't that clear through the clouds but the odd streaks that were visible were beautifully and delicately coloured. The rainbow reminded her of an archway through to another dimension. She sat there, letting her imagination wander, taking her into different worlds beyond the horizon. Once it was quite dark, she switched on the ignition and made her way to the next interview.

In spite of making an appointment, there was no reply. She looked impatiently at her watch, knowing that the next people wouldn't want her there early. They'd be in the middle of their dinner at this time of night. They'd told her that on the phone, so she didn't want to intrude or, indeed, upset them by barging in more than an hour before time. She'd try the one booked after that. If they weren't ready for her, there'd be no problem. She'd get back in the car and catnap for a bit, wet clothes and all.

The entire sky erupted as she drove back to the bay and the rain was discharged in sheets. So heavy was it that from time to time, she found it difficult to see the road, let alone follow it. Still, she reached the address, parked the car and having collected her clipboard and pen, made her way along the path.

It was much longer than she'd anticipated and the rain was running down her back and into her boots. Her hair was saturated, water dripping out of her fringe and running down her face. She was thoroughly uncomfortable and wished it would stop.

There was a single light on in the front of the house, the only illumination for what felt like miles. No street lighting. Nothing coming from the neighbouring homes. 'What a grim place to live,' she thought, and continued on down the path.

The door was concealed – nothing at the front and as she walked down the sideways, peering at brickwork, there was nothing obvious there, either. 'How long do I have to wander round this wretched place turning into one of the Walking Drowned?' she said out loud. What did that matter? There was no-one to hear her.

As she walked, the storm finally broke and whilst she'd never liked storms, it was accompanied by a let up in the rain, so it was a fair trade. She counted the time between strike and boom and knew it was getting nearer.

Suddenly, there was a massive bolt of lightning. It wasn't just loud, but supernaturally bright, covering the entire sky and if she hadn't been so frightened, the patterns made by the shivering flashes of electricity would have been magnificent to behold.

Making her way to the back of the house, she was positive she saw a unicorn, white and stately, unfazed by all going on around it. 'Poor thing must be drenched,' she thought, then recognised how stupid she was being. It couldn't possibly be real. 'It was that man put the idea in my head and my imagination's working overtime,' she scolded. As the flash faded, she stopped in her tracks, transfixed, staring at the darkness where she believed the animal had stood. Then, with a sigh of relief she realised it must be a statue. Yes, that was it. The millionaire recluse had a sculpture in her back garden and it had given rise to the folklore about her having a pet.

She knew she had to find the doorbell and talk to her clients, so pulled herself to and restarted her search. Another bolt and this time, the unicorn looked straight at her, their eyes meeting, each silently acknowledging the other. It was a moment that was over far too quickly. Darkness again. She resolved to forget the interview and go back to the car to ponder on what she'd seen. She was sure this time. It was certainly there and it was real.

She turned round and for the first time noticed the bench. She sat down, closed her eyes and slipped silently away.

HUGGING RABBITS

I'd fallen on my feet, that much was clear. This little house in my landlady's garden might have been tiny but it was now my home and all I had to do to pay the rent was to keep the dogs company while she and her husband were at work at night; and take 'the girls' for walks when they were too tired after a gruelling shift at the shelter. Emma's mother had lived there before. In fact, it was for her that they'd had it built, but she'd found herself a new husband – at the age of seventy eight – and moved in with him. No-one there now to look after the dogs, so they'd advertised. My friend Zoe had called my mobile, told me to apply; and here I was.

I hoped it was going to be short-lived and that once the fuss had died down, I'd be able to move back to Essex. Maybe not Epping Forest – too many memories – but that was where my life was – all my friends (or the people I had considered to be friends, many of whom still were but not all), the activities I'd so enjoyed, the work I'd been doing. I'd trained as a vet nurse. There was no need to earn a lot of money so I could follow my heart and that meant looking after animals. So, taking care of a couple of dogs shouldn't be too much trouble. And it wasn't. It was, though, therapeutic.

I didn't know Somerset at all. To me, it was somewhere to drive through on the way to Devon or Cornwall and in recent years, I hadn't done much of that, deciding to explore East Anglia instead, now that I was living there. I was glad it was somewhere totally unknown. It made me feel that I could be anonymous, could hide and disappear. I wasn't using my real name, of course. At least, I was, but it was my second name I called myself now and I'd never used my married name anyway, so no-one would identify me from that. My hair had been cut into a severe bob, rather than the long gentle waves that had become my trademark over the years; and dyed back to its natural colour. With everything that had happened, I'd lost a lot of weight, so it was easy to find an excuse to buy an entirely different wardrobe. Even Zoe didn't recognise me initially when she came over on my first weekend to see if I was settling in.

I was lucky in that having lived 'rent-free' for nearly eleven years with an allowance for household bills, which had run to keeping me in food and everything needed for the house, I'd got quite a little nest egg, so it didn't matter that much if I couldn't find a job in a hurry. When I spoke to Emma on the phone, I told her I hoped to get employment in an animal sanctuary and she said it would be fine, as long as I'd still be okay at night when the dogs needed someone around. Given that they did little beyond snore, there was virtually no care involved, but for me, it was heaven. I could spend the days exploring Somerset with a pooch on either side and give myself the chance to establish some sort of normal free from pressure.

I suppose I should tell you why I'd ended up in this position. Have you ever heard of Aidan Franklin? The Irish film star who moved to Hollywood and was notoriously private? Well, I met him when he was just a student at the local drama school. We were always close and got engaged when he finished his course but when his big break came, he took it; and why would he not? He moved over to the States, got very famous, made big bucks and after a couple of years, asked me to marry him, making it clear that the nature of his work meant that we'd be apart most of the time. It was all very low key and the only people who knew were those friends who could keep a secret. He didn't want his private life made public and if I'm honest, neither did I. I'd fallen in love with an unknown student and had no inclination for signing up as the wife of a star. He bought a beautiful five bedroomed house in the Forest, we furnished it together and it was here he lived when he came back to Britain, which wasn't that often. He was in demand all over the world and I didn't see him anywhere near as much as I would have liked but it worked for us. Until, that is, I saw the news and discovered he'd been killed in a motor cycle crash, leaving behind Birdie, the wife no-one knew he had.

***

After a couple of weeks of doing nothing but slobbing around the house, going for walks and sampling the local provender (and delicious it was, too) I went to the nearest library and used their internet to find out where the animal sanctuaries were. There had to be some. Sadly, there always are. And no, I couldn't use the laptop in the house, because according to Emma 'we're on St Michael's ley line here. It blocks the signal'.

There were three sanctuaries close enough for me to look for work, one of which was advertising for an assistant two days a week, the other two asking for volunteers. Volunteering would be fine. I could always try to get upgraded to 'proper staff' once I'd got my feet under the table, if, of course, I stayed in the area.

To cut a long story short, 'Dog Days' asked me to do a couple of shifts as a volunteer and then, if it worked out, they'd get references for me and see about offering me the job.

When the reference came through from my last employer, a lovely vet who knew everything but was very discreet and was obviously hoping that my move west would help sort me out, they were suspicious as to why I'd applied for a job 'cleaning up cat and dog mess when I was a fully qualified and experienced veterinary nurse'. I was prepared for this, and explained it was because I wanted to work in a sanctuary. In the past, I pointed out, I'd been told I was over-qualified and didn't want to be turned down again. 'So, when you've got the experience you're after, are you going to leave us in the lurch?' she asked. 'Of course not. I told you, I want to work in a sanctuary. Why would I leave a job if it was going well?' She seemed happy with this reply and I started working on Wednesdays and Thursdays, with the option of taking on extra days if anyone was sick or on holiday. Happy days were certainly in the offing.

***

The days after the news of Aidan's death were spent in a bit of a daze. I was sure they must have got it wrong. I mean, how on earth could he have a wife in the USA when he was married to me? And if that wasn't enough, how could this cold, hard-looking woman have captured his heart? He was so free and happy go lucky, not at all like this sour-faced diva whose picture was in all the papers and was seen all the time sobbing (without damaging her make-up, of course). I wondered if there were any kids but none were mentioned, so I assumed not.

I couldn't help thinking back to all the time we'd spent together wandering around the Forest, chatting about the future, planning for the time when he'd take on less work so we could be together more and live like a proper married couple. I wasn't insular, exactly, but I liked my own company and was perfectly self-sufficient. When he was away, seeing my friends and going to work suited me just fine. But when we were together – wow, it was blissful. Fame really hadn't changed him. He was still the lovely man I'd met at the Open Day at the drama school. Olympia (not her real name, as I expect you realise) had decided she wanted to train and asked me to go along with her to ask any questions she left out. In the event, she didn't get in but did go to another school, only to find that she didn't like acting after all.

We had a lovely dog, a little whippet called Sandy who'd been rescued from a house in Leyton after his owner had died suddenly and wasn't found for over a week. The poor little thing was beside himself, having to be dragged from the decaying body he was protecting and – we imagined – hoping he could coax back to life. We both loved that dog and whenever Aidan came home, he'd dance and sing with joy at being with him again. Sandy was every bit as enthusiastic.

I couldn't square any of this with the somewhat austere impression being given by the tabloids and TV reports of his life in LA. Surely this really wasn't Aidan. It certainly wasn't the man I knew. Maybe they'd got the wrong chap. Maybe if I could see the body, I could tell them this wasn't Aidan at all. It was someone else driving his bike. But I never got the chance. Birdie hadn't known about me, either, and when I called Aidan's phone and she answered, she refused even to talk to me, let alone attend his funeral and say my goodbyes.

It turned out he'd married her two months before he married me and hadn't left a will, so everything was hers, including the house in the Forest.

***

Life in Somerset was settling down well. I had my routine now and was beginning to make social contacts of my own. Zoe's friends were okay, but she, too, was a theatre person and I wanted to live a quiet life, not one revolving round first nights and other people's auditions. Not that they weren't nice people. They were. But there's something very calming about cleaning out pens and hugging rabbits. There was never any shortage of dogs to walk, cats to cuddle and hutches to clear out. Rabbits eat the first lot of faeces, you know. They've been half-digested and the second time it goes through their system, they get the optimum amount of nourishment. But maybe you'd rather not know that.

There was a very special rabbit called Boyzy, who had to be kept on his own, as the other males kept picking on him. We struck up quite a friendship and my first and last call of every day was to pick him up and have our now familiar, gentle interlude of silent communication. I was really pleased when he found a home but sorry to see him go. Still, that's what we were there for, to rehome pets, so although it was with a heavy heart I said goodbye, it was good to know he'd have all the love he deserved.

***

Birdie had decided she wanted me out of the house. It was hers. I had no right to it. I'd enchanted her husband and bewitched him into becoming a bigamist. Once the press got wind of it, it was hell. I'd lost Sandy a couple of weeks earlier and was grieving our lovely dog and now I had the paparazzi on the doorstep wanting to hear 'my side of the story'. I locked myself in but knew it would have to come to an end very soon, as I'd been given notice to quite in less than a week.

***

So that was how the person the press called Johanna Franklin turned into Izzy Bellingham and ended up in a tiny little house in someone's back garden. There are worse ways of living, you know. A five bedroomed house for a woman who was effectively single was a bit excessive, although I'd loved it at the time. And this place in Somerset gave me the same privacy and access to nature. With Emma and George's help, I'd put up bird boxes and feeders, made a picnic area outside and was getting stuck in with their vegetable patch and flower gardens. If that wasn't enough, there was a tawny owl nesting in one of the trees, the first time it had ever happened. Emma got me involved with the Bridgwater Flower Festival, which opened up all sorts of avenues, what with the diverse selection of people all doing their bit; and I was keen to get involved in the rejuvenation of the canal.

With no prior warning, I realised one afternoon that I was genuinely happy. The future didn't worry me anymore and the past was no longer painful. How fortunate am I?

***

On a typical afternoon at the Sanctuary, after walking the bigger dogs for their third outing of the day, I was making my way back to the main building to rest my feet and enjoy a cup of tea with my colleagues. Through the staff room window, I could hear raised voices.

'Leave her alone. She's been through enough and is obviously doing her best to build a new life and put all that other stuff behind her.'

'But I told you months ago she was Johanna Franklin! None of you would believe me.' The distinctive voice clearly belonged to Viv and sang out as loud and clear as a bell on Christmas Eve.

'Poor woman's been through hell. How would you feel if your husband died and to top it all, had another wife?'

'Oh for heaven's sake! Nothing's as clear cut as all that. There's a lot more to this than meets the eye,' replied Viv.

The conversation continued but I was unable to focus on anything more, so I went to the rabbit hutches and calmed myself down talking to my bunny friends. I decided the only thing to do was brazen it out, so I went back to the main building and made my way to the staff room, convinced that nothing would be said to my face.

As I walked through the door, Viv fixed me with her well-known stare, lifted up the paper with its photograph of me and the headline *Whatever happened to Johanna Franklin?* Clearly a slow news day.

'Well,' she demanded, 'what was it like being married – or more accurately, not married – to Aidan Franklin?'

***

I have no idea how I got home. I only remember sinking onto the sofa and putting my head in my hands.

I didn't hear the knocking on the door but was brought back to earth by Emma tapping on the window insistently until I lifted my head and invited her in. She had the dogs with her. Pansy was leaping around being propelled by her little tail; Hettie, always a little more restrained, gazed up at me with her tail wagging, tongue hanging out and ready to start licking my hands at the word 'okay', which her was her signal that kissing her aunt was permitted. I crouched down and let myself get lost in the joy of being with animals that didn't care who I was or where I came from.

'What's happened?' asked Emma, as she brought over two mugs of steaming hot chocolate.

My head went back into my hands again. I took a few deep breaths and sat up as straight as I could.

'I'm the woman they're calling Johanna Franklin.' I pronounced it as it should be, with the 'J' as a 'Y' – my mother's – German-Swiss – and aspirated the H. I said nothing more. Just waited for a shocked reaction. All she said was 'And?'

'I'm the woman who made Aidan Franklin a bigamist.' I said, not even hoping for the best.

'Izzy, do you really think we didn't know? Your disguise was a good one but no-one could mistake those eyes and nose. Your picture was everywhere. For a while you were probably the most famous woman in the country.'

'And you didn't care?' I asked, incredulous. She must have been the only person who didn't.

'Of course not. Not in the way you mean. We needed someone to look after the dogs and as possibly the best known veterinary nurse in the world, we figured we'd struck gold. Your personal life had nothing to do with us.'

So, here was someone who hadn't branded me as the Scarlet Woman – does anyone use that phrase anymore? – and who didn't care anyway. We sat in silence for a bit and then I asked 'does anyone else know?'

There was a pause before she answered 'most people, I expect, and there have been bits of gossip but the feeling is that without knowing your side of the story, we were in no position to point the finger. I imagine we've all done things that turned out to be errors of judgement, stupid, regrettable mistakes or whatever. It's just that not all of us ended up plastered over the newspapers as a result. To be honest, given that at the time they dubbed you "the reclusive wife not married to the reclusive film star", it was pretty obvious it wasn't the public eye you were ever interested in.'

'But until today, no-one has said a word.' And I recounted the exchange I'd heard through the window at the Sanctuary and Viv's almost triumphant display of the Daily Dirt.

'You know, Izzy, most people will be kind if you give them a chance. Of course, there'll be people rejoicing, wallowing in a large vat of schadenfreude, but they're the sad ones that haven't got enough to do with their time. You're lucky to have been able to keep out of their way until today, that goes without saying, but there's more support out there for you than you can possibly dream of.'

We chatted a bit about the Sanctuary and what I was going to do. The decision we made was that as I was due in again the next day, I'd get myself ready in the morning and go in as usual, like nothing had happened. 'After all,' she said, 'none of this was your choice. Why should you pay any more dearly than you already have?'

I felt tears welling up in my eyes but swallowed them down. 'So you mean you're not going to throw me out?' At this, she threw her head back and laughed. 'Good heavens!' she said. 'What on earth are you thinking? George and I have been trying to think of ways of enticing you stay for good. We know we're lucky to have found such a good dog sitter, gardener, caretaker, assistant cook and yes, friend, and we probably won't be so fortunate again. And all for living rent free in a property that would either have stood empty, needing to be cleaned and maintained regularly, which takes up an awful lot of precious time and cash; or knocked down. It wasn't cheap putting it up, so destroying it wouldn't have been the best option.'

'But you were advertising for a dog sitter!' I said.

Now it was her turn to look uncomfortable. 'No we weren't, Izzy. Zoe told us what had happened to you and asked if you could camp out in mum's old house. We cooked up that fiction between us to give you a purpose in being here.'

'So you knew Zo before?' I said, again incredulous.

'Of course, she works as a casual at the Shelter with George and me.'

I'd often wondered what she did to earn her living when she wasn't on stage. She never claimed to be doing anything other than act but she was one of those people who just floated through life without ever seeming to touch the sides.

'Can I ask you a question?' she enquired. In another life, I'd have been churlish enough to point out that she just had, but things were different now. 'In the storm that brewed after Aidan's death, did you ever get the chance to grieve?'

I realised I hadn't. Not really even for the loss of Sandy, who was now buried in the garden of Birdie's Epping Forest home.

'Would you like to talk about him?'

And that was it. I must have spent hours that evening, sobbing my heart out and remembering what a lovely bloke I'd been married to, or rather, not married to. That evening with Emma – and, of course, hugging rabbits – were the best therapy I could ever have had.

***

Work at the Sanctuary carried on as normal. No-one ever mentioned Viv's intrusive questioning and I'd started to feel as if this was where I belonged, looking after these unhappy charges, who (like me) were on the receiving end of misfortune. I'd often wondered why humanity can't be more like other animals and just accept each other for what we are; but I'll never have the answer to that. Somerset, too, was really working its magic and I no longer hankered after Essex. Various friends were being brave enough to come and visit, feeling that enough time had elapsed that they wouldn't be followed to see if they were going to see the infamous Johanna Franklin. We all agreed that the life I had was better than anything I would have been able to choose, given my earlier state of distress. I'd stopped thinking that the house was too small. There was only me, after all, and if I wanted a dog or cat, there'd be room.

George had helped me to turn a part of the garden into my own patch and erected a very low fence, so that the house appeared self-contained. Life was good.

When the auctioneers cleared out the furniture they'd collected from the Epping house, they found an envelope marked 'To be opened in the event of my death.' Well, they took it to the auction house solicitor, who opened it and found the Last Will and Testament of Aidan Franklin.

It transpired he'd left the house to me as well as everything else he had and any earnings accrued after his death. The one exception was the home his wife had been living in, as he didn't want to leave her without a roof over her head 'If Birdie had anything else,' it read, 'she'd only squander it and it won't take her long to find a replacement for me.' I felt almost sorry for her.

She contested the will – why would she not? – but lawyers on both sides of the Atlantic pronounced it to be water-tight.

It took some time for everything to come through, but when it did, I found myself to be truly wealthy. I gave a substantial amount to Emma and George, as 'lifetime's rent' on the house; a considerable amount to the shelter where they worked, securing its future for a good long time; and had the Aidan Franklin Rabbit House built for the Sanctuary, as well as giving them enough to keep them safe for many years to come. I'd love to tell you I put the rest to good use, but whilst I don't fritter it away, it's coming in handy to help out friends and charities and I have a life free from financial worry. What's really nice, though, is that indulgences are no longer a thing of the past. I'd love to say my 'philanthropy' is due to the fact that I'm a saint, but sadly, nothing could be further from the truth. I am, however, acutely aware that when I needed help, it was the kindness of strangers that got me through. It was time for some payback.

What I hadn't known was that at the end of his will, Aidan had stated 'If I die young or suddenly, investigate Birdie.'

This, apparently, had been the signal the LA police had been waiting for. There were 'discrepancies' with both the motorcycle and the eye witness reports but nothing could be proven. After a lengthy investigation, Birdie was found guilty of second degree murder. 'It was the best we could do,' the officer said when questioned by the US journalists, 'but a satisfactory outcome.'

Poor Birdie. And poor Aidan.

***

HUGGING RABBITS

She never got to serve her sentence, because she was taken to a 'secure facility' on account of the fact that she was believed to be suffering from some sort of psychosis. She kept raving about it was me who'd told her how to fix the bike, me who put her up to it. It'd all been my idea and nothing whatsoever to do with her, because after all, she loved him. But, as everyone knows, she and I were never aware of each other's existence before.

What do you think?

To Stefan Powell

SHALL WE TALK?

If I remember rightly, it's at the base of that pyramid, the one they taught us at school. Not Pavlov, the other guy. What on earth was his name? Similar to Pavlov. Oh well, if you remember – but I wouldn't blame you if you didn't – it's at the base of that with eating or drinking, one of life's essentials. Did you know, there are ninety six words for love in Sanskrit! Imagine! Ninety six! I wouldn't have thought there was enough of the stuff around to warrant ninety six words. But then, Sanskrit's a dead language so I guess it doesn't need to reflect real life. I wonder if it did back then. Come to that, did anyone ever speak Sanskrit?

Something else I remember from those heady days at school is that lots of living languages have a variety of words for it. There are four in Greek, eleven in Arabic. We Brits don't make distinctions though, we say we love our kids, we love our spouses, or our dog, or our clothes or a piece of music or – oh, you can fill in your own blanks. They're all different though. Not the same feeling at all. Nowadays, we say it all the time, so it's become more or less meaningless. It's different for the Germans, though.' A German says "Ich liebe dich", it's like they've given you a part of their soul. I think I prefer that. *'Love you babes.'* I doubt it.

Enough of that. For the first date – if it warrants the name – we went for a walk in the park. Wow! Fear and

SHALL WE TALK?

Trembling! How long do you think it took me to get ready? Certainly much longer than coffee, cake and a walk in the park demanded. I even wore make up, although frankly, no amount of industrial strength Pollyfilla would make any difference to the tramlines making pretty patterns over my glorious visage. It was sunny but a bit drizzly and my carefully blow-dried hair went curly but he didn't seem to notice or if he did, he obviously didn't care. Or was being too polite to comment. I only found out later that he doesn't usually eat cake. When we were young, he was a glutton for any sort of sugary indulgence, but all our tastes change. Even I can't pack them away like I used to, although you'd never know it from the waistline and the hips.

I've been doing some OU work. A five thousand word essay on "The implication of coral bleaching for shallow sea biodiversity". Interesting stuff. Of course, all this 'diversional romance, as my friend Jeannie calls it, made it rather more difficult to take the OU seriously, but it's too important to abandon. Can't let everything drop just because there's a man on the scene.

Finding each other again didn't change a thing. There were no gaps to be filled, no "if onlys" or "what ifs". It just gave me a glow and a warm feeling on getting up in the morning and the world seemed that little bit sunnier. It wasn't something I was expecting at all. Well, you don't, do you, not when you get to my age. It's all 'Knit and Natter' and tea dances. Tea dances! Honestly? What do they think we were doing when we were young? It was most definitely not a sedate waltz over a nice cup of Builders' Brew. But it was exciting and fun. Anyway, after a lifetime of caring for other people, it was good to have someone looking out for me, for once. It wasn't too bad with my father – my mother was around then, although it was very time-consuming, just the same. It didn't leave much time for romancing, that's for sure. It felt like I'd got to put that all on hold, and then when there was time again, well, it felt like the ship had sailed. A long time hence. And wouldn't be coming back to pick up late passengers.

We went to a donkey sanctuary for our second "date" and naturally, I wanted to adopt every animal in sight. He wasn't quite so enthusiastic but was happy to play the game and to be honest, I think he was just relieved to discover I'm not the kind of woman who wants to spend all the time shopping. Although I have to confess here, at the donkey sanctuary, I knocked my hat into one of the paddocks, so we had to do a recce of the local charity shops to replace it. Whoops!

There hasn't been a great deal of experience to draw on, so I really wasn't very nice to him in the early days. It was a wonder that he persevered. It's just that right from the start, he seemed so much keener than I was and I was still smarting from the Toy Boy. Ah. The Toy Boy. He was a lovely bloke and I really shouldn't call him that, but what else can I call him? Sonny? We were a really good match but he was way too young and – that's another story.

There are different challenges with someone when it's the second time round, but, we followed the unspoken rules – a phone call every day, emails, meeting up as often as a separation of a hundred miles would allow – all the things you'd hope for, really, but I just couldn't respond in the way he seemed to want. You know what I'm saying here, ladies. (And gentlemen, should you be interested). Making the Beast With Two Backs. You see, the dust from everything else hadn't settled properly, so I was really reluctant to take things any further. I'm not making excuses, but the Toy Boy – well, we wanted different things and yes, you've got it exactly right, he was much, much younger than you're imagining, so it would never have been something to commit to in the way he wanted; but he was good company and we clicked; and when we split up, there were emotional repercussions. You know how it is, every little thing reminds you of them and anyone even remotely similar, like if they've got the same colour hair or wear the same type of jacket, it just brings them crashing back into your mind; and it takes a long time to fade. Then along came the Gardener with Benefits. I used to think of him as Half-and-Half-Man, because he was as bronze as an Olympic medal down to the bum and white the rest of the way, a bit like those postcards you see of Englishmen on the beach. And the muscles! I never asked him if he ever does any working out. Probably not, not with a physical job and providing little extras. And he was just the diversion needed. It certainly led to a redefinition of pruning the roses, if you get my drift. Now, if that's what they had on offer at the library, rather than that lovely but somewhat passionless guy from the horticultural society, there'd be loads more takers for the talks on garden maintenance.

What a bolt from the blue Toy Boy was. And the gardener, of course, mustn't forget him. I'd never have thought I'd have it in me, if you'll pardon the pun.

SHALL WE TALK?

I've only got this year and next left at the OU, you know. I can't quite believe it. It seemed such a marathon haul when I started, but it's just zipped by. They say it does when you get older, but young people these days say the same thing. I'm concentrating on the oceans for this final part. They matter, don't they. Not that all the other things don't, of course, but now, in what my sister jokingly calls 'my dotage' (only partially joking, I suspect), I don't have to worry about where it'll all lead, I can just indulge myself. Who said there are no advantages to getting older? He or she was wrong!

It's so much more difficult than it was when I was young. We knew what the parameters were then and we may not have liked them but at least we recognised where the lines were drawn. Did you know, that 68% of 18-29 year olds in America consider that an invitation out for a drink is sexual harassment? Yep, you heard right. Sexual harassment. So one of them says 'fancy a drink?' and the other one hears 'the first chance I get, I'm going to jump your bones' and it all ends up in court. Gosh, it's so complicated! How on earth do they ever get it together? But it's not just that the rules have changed. It's such a different proposition for us now. We're not testing ourselves anymore, or learning how to live or, heaven forbid! looking for a mate. We've done all that. Well, not all of us have, but it's all about the here and now and making the most of what we've got, not if it's going to lead to a trip down the aisle. 'Take care of today and tomorrow will take care of itself.' That's what by little brother – little. I use the word ironically of course – keeps telling me. He's got two kids and three grandchildren now. Mind you, he did marry young – only I never really understood what he meant previously. He was right, of course.

Back to the point, the gardener – I made it clear to him it really was just sex, but he was determined to get more, and then when he finally realised there was nothing more to have, he got all nasty and called me names and tried to make me feel bad about myself. No chance. You don't get to my stage in life without having to do a lot of basic surviving and being called names by the GwithB wasn't going to throw me off kilter. So when I said "it's only sex", what he heard was "try harder".

"How to look 10 years younger without surgery". Really? Even with the surgery it's a bit of a challenge if you're not going to look like a frightened snake. Who decides what to put in these magazines?

Pippa – she's my friend from the Brownies, so we've known each other a long time. Do the Brownies still exist? If they do, they're probably called something like "Unisex Pioneers" or "Small Adults for World Domination". And I bet they don't do Washing Up Badges anymore, more likely to be Rocket Mechanics for Beginners. Pity. The Washing Up Badge was the only one I got. Anyway, Pippa. She's always on the lookout for love. She says she's looking for raw, animal sex, and so she is, but that's only part of the story. As soon as she's actually doing the business, all of a sudden, she's in lurv and nothing can stem the flow. The rest of life is on hold and simply has to wait. That's where our hormones lead us, ladies! Whereas a chap, he says he loves you because he thinks if he doesn't, he won't be able to gain entry to your underwear. It's the twenty first century, for heavens' sake! He's more likely to find his way into your knickers by simply saying "I want to get inside your knickers". But then, that most likely wouldn't work for the likes of Pippa, so he tells her loves her, and what she hears is "you're the centre of my world and all the rest of my life's stopped mattering", which is, of course, what she means when she says it. She's had a really hard time with men, right through from a husband who knocked her about, one night stands, computer dates, live in lovers – the lot, you name it, she's done it and every single one has ended in disaster. Poor Pippa. If only she could hear "I'm after your body", she'd save herself an awful lot of heartache.

He gave me a free choice of things to do for a few days away, so we went for a trip on a narrowboat. Yep. You heard right. A narrowboat. You can't get much more up close and personal than a narrowboat. So, we hired one on the Oxford Canal, as there aren't any tunnels and I hate tunnels. It's very twisty and turny and we had a few, shall we say, interesting encounters with river banks and low bridges. Of course, there aren't many places for you to hide when you want a bit of privacy in a vessel 32ft long and 6 feet 10 inches wide, so it's a good job that we were at that point when privacy wasn't a major issue. You get into a completely different state of being on a narrowboat. It's so slow and tranquil and you feel as if you're part of nature, not just observing it. Everything's so close. You can smell it all, touch it, feel it against your skin, simply let yourself merge into it. It'd be good to it again one day. Maybe see if Pippa would like to come with me.

He's a terrific cook. I didn't have to do anything for the whole time we were away and we had hardly any provisions on board at all. It wasn't until we got back that I found out that he hates water, as he nearly drowned once. But he came with me, all the same. Aren't I a lucky woman?

Looking after my mother was tough. It wasn't so much that she was demanding, more that she took up a lot of time and would never be open about what she wanted, so I had to second-guess all the time. She always had to be top dog, no matter what was happening for me, and it shattered my dreams more times than you can count in a bag of beans. I don't think it was conscious, but it was definitely deliberate. You know what I mean – she pretended she was thinking of me, trying not to put on me, but underneath it, she was trying to prove she ruled the roost. She thought I owed her for bringing me into the world, and she believed I thought that, too. Poor mum. When it finally came to a head, she told me she thought I actually wanted to throw my own life away to look after her, although she didn't exactly use those words. We never did get on but we got over that debacle and by then it was too late to start again anyway. I told her "okay, I'll make sure you're safe" and she heard "I want to devote my entire life to your care". I got on with looking after her and she assumed that's that the way I wanted it. So, normal services were resumed.

He took care of me in ways I'd never experienced before, like my OU work. Most people think I'm mad, at my age (sorry, but these individuals are always banging on about 'my age' – which, incidentally, is very similar to theirs – and you sort of absorb it). Anyway, taking on a degree 'at my age'. They all tell me there's no point, not now. There's no chance of a career anymore. The thinking is that I did all those years nursing and that should be enough. But it really wasn't like that. I don't like to admit this, but I went into nursing because I was scared of being out of work and nurses, well, they're always in demand, aren't they. I'm not saying I didn't do it well or that I didn't enjoy it, but I wasn't an angel, although lots of people told me I was. So the OU – it's opening up a whole new world and I wonder if some people are a bit jealous, because I'm passionate about something new and they're not. He's not like that though. He thinks it's wonderful to be branching out. And he's interested in it, too, so we talk about it. The upshot was I started to relax, to want to give him more and let him in. So I told him, and what he heard was "I want you to dump your life and your autonomy and put me slap bang in the centre of your universe". Which wasn't what I meant at all. So anyway, after my declaration, he started to pull away. Surprised? No, nor was I.

One afternoon, we went to the river to feed the ducks. The sun was glinting off the water looking more like twinkling stars than the real things ever do; and the ducks were quacking and gobbling up the bread and squabbling between themselves about who knows what but seemingly happy in their ducky world. It was crisp and bright, and so, so peaceful. There aren't many times in life when we glimpse heaven, but that afternoon we did. And he told me he loved me. And what I heard was "I've got you where I want you. I can do what I like now".

So, that was the end of that.

TEACHING MANDARIN

Emer was really worried about the biology lesson that morning. 'For heaven's sake,' she said to herself on the way to school. 'I'm the secretary and my degree is in Mandarin.' The Head hadn't wanted her to cover those lessons, though. 'Your degree was twenty years ago,' she told Emer. 'You've forgotten most of it.'

'I remember more Mandarin than GCSE Biology,' had been Emer's retort, thinking 'I know where my nose is and that I have five fingers, but that's about it.' The Head, though, was adamant.

'Timetabling,' she'd said. Emer didn't bother to reply but wondered exactly what the timetabling implications would be if the secretary were taking a Mandarin class rather than a biology class. 'Naff all,' was her conclusion.

In the staffroom over break, she looked around her and wasn't surprised to see a cohort of teachers all looking frazzled.

'She's got me teaching chemistry,' said Jason, the Head of English. 'And Donna's been allocated to P.E.' Donna was nowhere to be seen. Emer's suspicion was that she was probably still in the gym area, attempting to work out what the different pieces of equipment were for. Clearly they bore no relation to the apparatus she routinely utilised to distil water or separate the different elements combined together to form a compound. 'Mind you, poor Alf's having to teach maths and it's not really what you expect when you take on a caretaking job, is it?' Jason stormed out into the playground and screamed. Was it even legal? Emer wondered.

***

'Diversification', the Head had informed the entire school during assembly. 'We all need to be more flexible. We're getting stuck in a rut and that's why our OFSTED report was so terrible, to say nothing of the exam results,' she'd said.

'A rut? At eleven years old?' Emer heard Katie whisper behind her and felt inclined to agree. 'And the exam results weren't that bad. Not compared with the way they used to be.'

Cooper, a particularly lively thirteen year old put his hand up and, surprisingly, had been allowed to pose his question. Maybe this, too, was part of the new order. Allow the students the chance to exercise their curiosity. 'Does that mean we can bring our Beano's into class Mrs Bradley?' he'd enquired.

'Fair question, young man.' Emer suspected that this was the Head's chosen form of address because she couldn't remember any of their names but had never voiced the opinion. 'But no. You are here to learn and the Beano provides no such opportunity.' There was a gentle sniggering among Cooper's classmates. 'Good try, mate,' said his neighbour. And assembly continued with the singing of the school song, as pretentious and lacklustre an offering as a tarnished silver-plated spoon.

***

'Is Mrs Bradley going mad, miss?' Emer was tempted to reply that yes, she was, and because of that they all had to be especially kind and understanding but realised in time that it probably wasn't the answer she should be giving.

'She's trying some educational experiments, Cooper,'

she said instead. The truth was she didn't have a clue what was going on in Mrs Bradley's brain. She could only hope it would mend itself very quickly.

'Like the ones we used to do where you spit into a test tube and see if the stuff at the bottom makes it turn black, miss, that sort of thing?' Emer wasn't sure if he was making it up to amuse his friends or genuinely trying to make sense of what was becoming an increasingly confusing school term; and this was a biology lesson after all.

'I don't really know. I'm not a teacher, you see, I'm a secretary, and we didn't do many experiments in my Mandarin degree.'

'Would you like to be a teacher, miss?' asked Levi.

'Not really. That's why I became a secretary.'

'I want to be a biology teacher, miss. Would you like me to take the class? We could say it's an educational experiment of our own.'

So that's how 9C ended up having an excellent lesson on the functioning of the kidney delivered by one of their own in total silence, not a single dissenting voice or aimlessly wandering body for the entire hour.

Maybe Mrs Bradley wasn't quite so mad after all.

***

Emer flicked through the TV schedule that evening to see if there was anything she could watch to help her in her new found occupation – not found by her, unfortunately – either for her own teaching or to sit the students in front of for an hour. She'd never realised before how long it could take for sixty minutes to elapse and that's how she was thinking of these time periods, because it sounded so much shorter put like that. But no, the closest she could find was a programme about big animals eating smaller animals and that didn't seem right, not in a school where half the kids were vegetarian. She decided to go in really early the next morning to see if she could catch Ben and ask him to give her some idea of what he would like her to teach. It was his lessons she'd been allocated to and when he eventually took them back again, he'd want them to be up to date.

Ben, though, was having problems of his own. He'd been told to teach Spanish and he'd never spoken a word in his life. 'Sorry Emer, I'd love to help you but I just haven't got time. I got onto Youtube yesterday evening to see if I could get any useful information from there and although there are pages and pages of it, none of it helped me much.'

Emer walked past his class when it was about fifteen minutes in. There were twelve year olds chatting and reading comics, wandering round the room and playing games on their phones. Ben was clearly shaken and at a loss.

'8B,' he said for the umpteenth time, 'we have a lot to do today. Please take your seats and get out your books.' But there was so little conviction in his words, the only response was total disdain.

'Oy. Listen up you morons.' Phoenix, a dainty girl who looked very much like she'd fall over if someone coughed two streets away, was standing at the front of the class with her hands on her hips. 'Sir's doing his best. Issnot 'is choice to be stuck 'ere in the Spanish classroom instead of the bio lab. Wind yer necks in, sit down and listen to Sir!' To Ben's surprise, they did.

'Now then Mr. Davy, if you can't teach us Spanish, it'll have to be a biology lesson.' Phoenix returned to her seat and gave him an encouraging smile.

Ben was surprised he hadn't come up with that particular solution himself. 'But what about Mrs Bradley?' he queried.

'You leave her to us, sir,' said Phoenix, narrowing her eyes and raising her brows.

So, he improvised a lesson on how cells make proteins, with class members acting the parts of the unravelling DNA in the nucleus, messenger and transfer RNA and amino acids, culminating in a glorious string of protein. If he said so himself, it was a very successful lesson.

***

Back in her study, Mrs Bradley was enjoying the mayhem she had caused. 'Nothing like a shake up to revitalise the brain cells,' she told herself. True, the staff room was a place to be avoided these days but then she often thought it was unbecoming to take tea with the teachers. After all, they probably wanted a good bitch, like she had when she was at the chalk face and her presence could only get in their way.

When she opened the study door after it had been rapped upon particularly viciously, she was somewhat surprised to see a deputation of students, one from each year group.

'We wanna word wiv' you, miss,' said Levi barging his way past her, leading a gaggle of rampaging students into the splendour of the oak panelled room. Taken aback, Mrs Bradley gingerly made her way to her chair and sat down behind her desk.

'What can I do for you?' she requested.

'Well, it's like this. We're 'ere for our education. You tell us that once a week in assembly. Well, we ain't getting no education wiv all our teachers doing stuff they know nuffin' about. We want our lessons back.'

Mrs Bradley stifled a smile and assured the group that they would, indeed, find that things would be back to normal the next Monday. She was as good as her word.

Walking round the school glancing in to the different classrooms, she was delighted to observe that the students were all behaving impeccably and the school had turned into a model of how things should be.

'Good,' she said to herself, 'it worked. I thought once they discovered how lucky they were to have such excellent teaching staff, they'd appreciate them and knuckle down to learn.'

The success of the experiment was reflected both in the exam results and the OFSTED report.

***

If you think that's crazy, take a look at what's been happening in education over the past fifty years.

CONSULTATIONS
PART 1

Week 5

'Good morning. Please, sit down. Make yourself comfortable. How are you feeling today?'

'I'm doing okay, thanks. How are you?'

'I, too, am fine. Thank you for asking. But we're here to talk about you.' *Same ritual every week. Be prepared for the questions about Alice and the kids. Let's forestall.* 'And my wife and children, they too are doing well. Thank you. Now, is it okay for us to get back to the reason why you're here? How are you feeling?'

'Fine. Just fine. Except for the tiredness, of course. Still can't sleep. You know how it is. You toss and you –'

'Let me stop you there. Do you remember that last week' *and the week before and the week before* 'we talked about how the insomnia is the symptom, not the cause?'

'Well, yes, but it's the insomnia that's causing everything to go wrong. The tiredness. The feeling of being drained and not being able to keep my eyes open for the fatigue. It wears you out. Hahaha! Did you hear what I said then? Being worn out wears you out! Hahahaha!'

'Very amusing, yes. Now, let me ask you another question *for about the hundredth time*. When you are unable to sleep, tossing and turning, or even just lying quietly in bed doing the exercises we discussed' *my turn to laugh now. Who was it who talked about the triumph of hope over experience?* 'what are you thinking about?'

'Well, I'm thinking about not being able to sleep. How tired I'll be in the morning. How it'll be at work with me having to fight against falling asleep all the time. How many coffees I'll have to drink to keep me awake all day. That sort of thing.'

'Ah. *Probably worth finding out a bit about his caffeine intake.* You haven't previously mentioned the coffee. How many would you say you drink during the course of the day?'

'Well, I suppose about ten, really. One every hour and then there are two at lunchtime. So, yes. Probably ten. And then I get one on the way home, so that's eleven. And one on the way in, twelve.'

Holy horseshit! There must be a shortage of coffee in his part of the City! 'I think you could consider cutting down on the coffee. Maybe one cup on your way in and one at lunch time. And have a light lunch, not something that is going to fill your stomach and make you sleepy and sluggish.'

'Wow. That's not much coffee. You're a hard taskmaster, you know. Is that "one in the morning" just one at home, instead of getting one on the way in? I drink a pot before I even leave the house. Shall I just have that?'

CONSULTATIONS

Bloody hell! 'I think maybe just have one cup of coffee with a light breakfast before you leave for work. You might find it helps. Now, I think we should return to the question of what might be concerning you that is causing you to lie awake at night. How are things with Shelby?'

'They're okay. We get along just fine. She gets a bit tetchy with me at times, because I'm so tired and don't want to do anything. I mean, at the weekend, she asked me to mend the shed door to stop it banging all night' –

Right. Now we have an outhouse door slamming on a regular basis during the hours of darkness. I wonder if the neighbours get any sleep or if they, too, will be knocking on my door seeking solutions. This gets better and better.

-'but I was too tired, what with not sleeping and everything. She really lost her rag.'

'Well, as a start, do you think it might help things if you mended the door? See if that makes any difference?' *When did I become a DIY advisor?*

'Blimey you're as bad as she is. I'll have a go on Saturday. That do you?'

'And how are things at home aside from the shed door?'

'They're fine.'

Silence. The clock is one of those modern ones that makes no sound at all. The doctor can

hear himself breathe. In spite of that, it Is not uncomfortable but companionable and calm.

'Blimey doc, I nearly fell asleep then. Just shows how tired I am. It's cosy in here, isn't it, and makes you feel calm and restful.'

'I think so, yes. Can you think of any reason why it might not be so at home in your own bedroom?'

'Well, I suppose the shed door might make a difference! Hahahaha!'

'And is that all? You mentioned that Shelby gets a little tetchy because of your tiredness. Do you think there might be something else going on between you to cause tension?'

'Well of course I'm going to be tired. I don't sleep. Can't you just give me some pills?'

'I could prescribe pills, yes, but that would not be appropriate. Your GP can prescribe you pills, which I understand she has done in the past to no avail. We are trying here to uncover the reason that you are unable to sleep and see if you can find ways of putting things right.'

Silence. The doctor studies the client's face and tries to read something in it but it is blank. The client studies his nails and stifles several yawns.

'We only have five minutes left, I'm afraid. The homework this week is a little different from the norm. What I would like you to do before our next meeting is to cut down on the coffee, mend the shed door and also speak to Shelby about how she feels.'

'Blimey, doc! She'll chew my ear off for the best part of a day!'

'Nevertheless, I think it might be a way into looking at how you feel yourself.'

'If I must. Have a good week.'

'You too.' *Relief.*

The doctor writes up his notes, settles down for a couple of minutes calm breathing and gets ready for the next client.

Week 6

'Well, I did my best to mend the shed door only it still keeps on banging. Cut down on the coffee. I even tried those things about concentrating on my breathing and different bits of my body. Didn't help though. Made me feel horny and Shelby got really brassed off with me and went and slept in the spare room.'

'And how did that make you feel?'

'Well, I wasn't happy. I mean, she's my wife. I know this is the age of the Liberated Woman but if a man has needs she should respect that, not flounce off next door and leave him to it.'

'So this annoyed you, yes?'

'Well wouldn't it annoy you? You can tell me doc, you know, man to man.'

'We're not here to discuss my feelings but yours.'

'All this banging on about feelings! I thought you were going to help me with my sleep not try to turn me into a weakling! I've got responsibilities. A good job. People rely on me to keep the department going. I can't do that dog-tired, now can I?'

Ah. Genuine anger. Maybe a bit of progress. 'So how are you feeling now?'

'Like I'd like to take a swing at you! Not that I would, of course. Don't think that.'

Thank god for that. Personally, I don't mind being a 'weakling', especially if it means I avoid a broken nose.

'But honestly, doc, none of this is helping.'

'I'd like to talk about you and Shelby. Would you say you are happily married?' *Well, he didn't answer the last dozen times you put the question so what are the chances now?*

'We were before I got this problem with my sleep.'

Oh god. Someone shoot me! 'And how does it show, this unhappiness you are experiencing now as a result of the turn of events at home?'

'Well, she bangs around all the time. Goes out every night with her mates. Won't have sex with me. Says it's all I want her for and she thinks she deserves more than that...'

Okay. Let's ignore the fact that I asked about him and his answer has been about her; and that he had the legitimate opportunity to remind me that he doesn't sleep and didn't take it. 'And is she right? Is that all you want her for?'

'Well it is now. I mean, you can't exactly have fun with someone who wants to talk about her problems all the time, can you?'

'And what is it specifically she wants to talk about?' *Maybe this will be an entry into the emotional atmosphere in the home. Flying pigs alert!*

'Well, she's not happy. Says it's my fault. My fault! Can you believe that? Says I never want to do anything anymore but how can I? How can I do anything when I'm always so bloody tired?'

'And do you talk to her about how she feels, as we suggested last week you might?'

'Not likely! I mean, my job wears me out. She just teaches in a primary school. How hard can it be making Teletubbies out of playdough and planting potatoes all day for 'healthy school dinners'? It's okay for her. She's got it easy.'

'And is this how she feels also?'

'Course not. But we're supposed to be talking about me and my feelings!'

Alleluia! 'Indeed we are. So let's get back to the matter in hand. You appear to be angry at the situation in your home and not at all happy with the turn your marriage is taking.'

'You're putting words in my mouth. I never said that.'

'No, but as you are unable or unwilling to tell me how you feel, I have to try to interpret the things you are telling me. You are always welcome to correct me if I'm wrong. This is week 6 of a series of twelve sessions. I'm thinking that maybe we should postpone the final six sessions until you feel better able to talk to me about the things that are troubling you.'

'You can't do that, doc! These sessions are for me, to sort out my insomnia!'

'Actually, I can. I want to help you but don't believe my input is having the slightest impact. I think it might be better for you to have a break and decide what you would like to do.'

'Can't you just give me some sleeping pills?'

'Absolutely not. And I am also not going to respond to any more comments about your tiredness, not today and not when we resume our sessions. If, between us, we are to find a way to help you, we have to discover why you are not sleeping because that is the problem. The insomnia is the effect, not the cause.'

> **Silence. The client stares at his feet, occasionally sighing and biting his nails. The doctor watches him closely, deciding to allow the client to break the silence rather than him stepping in.**

'At work yesterday, Janice – she's my secretary – she made a complaint about me. Said I'd snapped at her and made her feel small. I didn't know I'd done it. Honestly I didn't. I couldn't find a file and when I asked her to look for it, she went to the filing cabinet and there it was. She giggled and said it was an easy mistake to make. I mean, I told her off, of course I did, but she shouldn't speak to me like that. And now – now, well, I tried to tell Shelby. Tried to talk to her. To tell her that I was in trouble at work and all she said was "well now you're in trouble at home, as well, because I'm leaving you."'

> **The client looks at the doctor, his face in a fixed expression that might be interpreted as terror. The doctor makes no such assumption, knowing how difficult it is to accurately read what someone is feeling from a facial expression. He again decides to let the client break the silence.**

WEEK 6

'I can't manage without her doc, I really can't. I – I – '

The client breaks down in tears. The doctor hands him a box of tissues and allows him to cry himself out.

'Help me, doc, please.'

'Of course. Talk to me about Shelby. Would you like to do that?'

'Please doc. Yes please.'

GRANNIE LOUIE'S BIG ADVENTURE

Part 2: The UDD

'This is the last photograph we have of Grannie Louie before she disappeared.' Jake handed over the small square of paper. They'd taken it off one of the posters made at the time asking anyone who knew anything to come forward. No-one had. There'd been no sightings, no body found, nothing. The young woman sitting opposite him took it and studied it carefully.

'You're not still looking for her, are you? She's long gone.' Freddie had never known his great-grandmother. How could he? He wasn't even an idea when she'd gone missing. 'Why don't you just leave it alone? She caused enough bother by going off like that at the time without putting all the rest of us through it now.' Freddie was home for the long vacation, the last one before his clinical studies began and he'd be working a full week all year.

Jake could see his point. Josie and Rick had never recovered from her unceremonial departure and he and India felt as if they'd lost their parents as well as their Grannie.

'Would you mind if I took the dossier away with me?' the young woman asked. 'In the Unsolved Disappearances Department, we can find things that the layman can't.

'By all means,' said Jake, giving her the box file.

'Good riddance,' said Freddie. 'I, for one, never want to hear anything about her again.'

PART 2: THE UDD

Back on the ship, they were all watching carefully, checking that there was nothing that could give them away. 'Do you think one of us should go down there?' asked Hidrah (147, as he was known in the community). 'The interest in this has never waned.'

'Better not,' said Kaydock – 167. 'We don't want to arouse suspicion and by this point, there could be a lot more of them sensitive enough to see us and penetrate our disguises.' They all agreed that most of the "disappearances" hadn't caused this much anguish. They only ever invited those individuals to join them who genuinely wanted to leave and never put any pressure on the people they chose. Theirs was a happy ship and not a single newcomer had ever regretted leaving the old life behind. Indeed, Grannie Louie had fitted in like she'd been born to it. She loved the company – all of them intelligent with a wide range of interests, good fun and easy to get on with – and the lifestyle: who wouldn't enjoy travelling round the universe in a luxurious space ship so full of leisure facilities it would take her several earth lifetimes to sample them all. She only had to decide she definitely wanted something, think about it in the right way and it happened. It did mean she had to be careful what she thought, but she'd got used to that very quickly.

***

Jake knew that at this point, there was little chance of ever finding out what had happened to Grannie Louie; and Freddie was right. It had shattered the family unit and as a result, they'd all suffered. Jake never did his Sports Science degree; India had missed out on her nurse training. For him, the sad thing had been that he adored his Grannie

GRANNIE LOUIE'S BIG ADVENTURE

Louie and he couldn't help thinking that if he hadn't made that comment about her losing her marbles, none of it would ever have happened. He'd been the trigger, of that he felt sure. Still, no point in dredging all that up again. But there was absolutely no doubt in his mind at all: if there was any way he could find out what had happened to her, he had to pursue it.

***

The young woman from the UDD was poring over the contents of the box file. She found newspaper cuttings, adverts from newsagents' posters made by both the police and the family. They'd tried hard to find Grannie Louie and it was clear from all the other artefacts that they'd missed her terribly and had wanted her back. That last photo showed her sitting in the garden. She supposed that all the other family members had been cut out and this tiny image was showing her having a fun time celebrating someone's birthday, if the cake was any guide. Maybe even her own birthday. How old would she have been then? 71? 72? Difficult to tell from a photo. What was clear was that Grannie Louie had been happy. You could tell if someone was genuinely happy and not just putting on a face for the camera. This was a picture of a woman content with her lot.

***

The crew of the ship were getting concerned.

'What if asking Grannie Louie to join us was a mistake?' asked Kaydock (167) over their meal.

'She's had a wonderful time – still is. How can you suggest she'd have wanted it any other way?' Mithram – otherwise

PART 2: THE UDD

known as 101 – was the most hedonistic of them all and felt that they should be a little less keen to condemn their well-meant actions. 'She had a free choice. She made the decision she made because she wanted to join us.'

'But her family suffered so badly.' This came from Lindel, one of the veterans of the community (no longer in need of a number) who'd seen it all before and was concerned when things were difficult for the newcomers. 'They missed her such as lot, and well, maybe Grannie Louie feels some of that, too. Or maybe more. Maybe she regrets the suffering caused and feels wrong about it.'

They'd have to ask her.

The investigation wasn't exactly ongoing. Everyone knew that there was no hope of ever finding out what had happened but Jake and his sister India were still grieving. It was only fair to give them the very best chance to heal. What could she tell them? That she hadn't wanted pills to stop her seeing the men, so she'd chosen to take her chances and go with them? That she fancied an adventure and hadn't realised she'd love it so much that there'd be no return? She'd had lots of opportunities to come back and they could have dropped her at exactly the same moment as she'd left. No-one would have been any the wiser. No, they hadn't forced her to stay there but she revelled in every moment and had wanted to stay. If she went back to the house now and said 'I'm your Grannie Louie,' they'd think she was even barmier than they had back then but worse, they could think she was deriding them. They'd certainly never believe that this young, vibrant woman was their lost grandmother. Grannie Louie, (or 273, to give her her new name) closed the file and returned to the house.

'Sorry,' she said. 'We did our best but I'm afraid this is a case that we'll never be able to close.'

'Oh well, thanks for trying,' said Jake and closed the door behind the gorgeous creature that in another life he'd have done his best to seduce. Another life? What was he thinking? 'There is only this one,' he thought. 'Or is there something else? Grannie Louie thought she'd seen visitors from space. Maybe she was right!' He chuckled to himself and poured another glass of wine. 'Maybe I'm losing my marbles, too,' he said.

When Grannie Louie – 273 – got back to the ship, she went to the crew room and asked them to close the file. 'You were right. He's a perfect candidate,' she said. The crew spruced themselves up and got ready for a visit to *The Earl of Southampton*.

It's not about finding your voice, but giving yourself permission to use it.

Kris Carr

PART 2

THE WILDERNESS YEARS

I was voice-less for sixteen years. Once I'd accepted that that was the case, the only option available was to build another life without it. Easier said than done, but it happened.

My neighbour and I shared an allotment which ran along the back of our two gardens. She cultivated the vegetables and I the fruit, as I was working and she wasn't. Veg takes a far greater input than fruit (at least it did for us) as I discovered that as long as the plants are kept watered, they'll thrive. It's possible, of course, that my lovely neighbour, Rene, did a lot of weeding and tending to my plants while I was out at work, but she never said so and no-one ever spilled the beans (pardon the pun). I loved seeing the plants grow from nothing into food we could eat, as well as being lovely to look at. In those days, too, there were many more bees and butterflies around and it was always a joy to be outside with them. Summer is simply not as welcoming without the hum of insects. As well as that, coming home from work and going to the allotment to see what was out there to form my meal was something I treasured. We weren't fully self-sufficient but didn't have to buy much. I've been a vegetarian since I was nineteen – most of that time vegan – so eating home-grown, freshly picked food was a bit like eating heaven.

The best thing that entered my life during this time was the Wildlife Trust. It opened up several different avenues and enabled me to learn things hitherto undreamt of and meet some lovely new people. One of these was Tony, who was the main Birding Guide and a lot of fun to be with. He took me to far flung places I'd never heard of, taught me how to watch birds rather than simply recognising them and gave me some pointers regarding learning song. This last – which I'd rather arrogantly thought would be straightforward for a one-time musician – turned out to be an extremely difficult business, and one that I'm still grappling with. He knew a lot about butterflies and moths, wild flowers and wild food. Happy days indeed.

Tony and I would meet early in the morning, drive off somewhere and spend the day seeking out the local flora and fauna. Sometimes we'd find a pub to have lunch in, others when we (or rather he) knew we'd be in the wilds of nowhere, we'd take a packed lunch and find somewhere to sit and enjoy it. I tried not to talk about the loss of my voice or anything to do with my time singing, but sometimes it just popped out. Tony didn't question and neither did he criticise or belittle my experience. As we got to know each other better, I realised that he understood far more than he let on but never found out why. This was the first time I felt that there was anyone out there interested enough to care.

I got involved with surveys, learning how to seek out the animal population without disturbing it, do accurate counts and learned a fair amount about statistical analysis. I did an Environmental Science degree (I have far too many educational qualifications, to which anyone who's read *Wyddershyns* will testify) and toyed with the idea of a research degree but didn't want to be pinned down to the study of a tiny fragment of the whole. If honest, I'd say I didn't really like the idea of becoming an expert in anything and still don't. There's much too much of interest out there to side-line such a vast majority of the whole; but as well as that, I didn't want to risk being that totally identified with anything ever again.

There was also a certain amount of educational work involved, not as much as I would have liked as I didn't want to work with children and spreading the word among the young was a big part of the brief for all the Trusts, for very good reason.

***

I continued reading everything I could about voices, still keen to learn what had happened to my own and why. There's a mahoosive amount known about the human voice and how it's produced. Fascinating stuff. At one point, I applied for training as a Speech and Language Therapist but was told that there was no guarantee I would be able to work solely with adults. For this reason, I didn't pursue the course. The idea of starting again in a new career at considerable expense, both financial and personal, only to find I had to do something I was totally unsuited for just didn't appeal. It was another blow, but having lost my singing voice, it was pretty small fry.

My speaking voice recovered during this period and I discovered that I could bypass the pain in my throat when acting and reciting. It was partly this that made me believe that whilst the original loss of voice was physical, not getting it back was psychological and emotional but I couldn't pin down why this should be and got no closer to being able to sing again.

There are a number of different factors involved in the possible emotional/psychological basis for not regaining my voice. This isn't an autobiography and I have no interest in providing a blow by blow account of where my psyche might have let me down. Or maybe it was me who let IT down. One of those things I'll never know.

During this time, I worked with Rod, an ex-footballer who'd had to retire due to a knee injury. Much to my surprise, there was someone who understood exactly what I was going through. As is frequently the case in this type of situation, when I was with Rod, there was no need – not even any desire – to talk about what had happened and nothing to be gained by trying to understand, but things felt better just for knowing that I was no longer alone with my pain.

***

There were benefits to this loss of voice, although I didn't recognise it at the time and think it unlikely I could have acknowledged it even if the realisation had been there. It's possible that these benefits were part of the cause of the continued lack of an instrument but it's as unknowable as everything else.

In the first place, life was much less 'fraught'. There was no longer any necessity to have every shade of emotion close to the surface so it could be called upon when needed for song. This kept things on an even keel. Living on high octane emotion all the time really isn't much fun, although again, at the time I'd never realised this was something I was doing.

Things were more predictable and considerably less disciplined. Much of a singer's time is spent protecting the voice, even though a lot of it becomes habit and unconscious. With no voice to protect, I could relax. There was more freedom in my social life, there being no need to avoid social occasions when there was an important performance imminent, no necessity to worry about overuse and fatigue, and although such hazards as cigarette smoke were – and are – unpleasant, they weren't a threat anymore. My diet, too, relaxed – there are lots of foods that affect our vocal chords. Late nights were more commonplace and getting tired was, in general, not such a big deal.

There were other things that came out of this period, too, not as obvious but just as real. I started learning Hindi, something I'd wanted to do since my late teens. I didn't get very far, as there was no-one to practice with but also because for some reason, the script looks to me as if it should be read from right to left, whereas it's left to right; and I never got into my head that I was trying to read it backwards. Very little was learned but all the same it was good to have a go. I also spent long hours walking in the forest for pleasure and took to using Shanks's pony instead of the car. Anything up to a five mile round trip was done on foot, up to ten miles on the bike, which over time extended to eight miles on foot and twenty miles on two wheels. I swam every day, something I could do now – there was no hope of singing anyway, so how much the chlorine in the swimming bath water affected my throat and chest didn't matter anymore. I loved – still do – the feel of my muscles and joints moving me through the air or water and the sensation of both mediums on my skin. I guess as a musician whose instrument is her own body, it's not that surprising that pleasures of the flesh rank so high. I was probably fitter during this time than at any other in my life.

Something I found hard was that so many people had intact voices, yet either claimed they couldn't sing – even though they never bothered to try and certainly never looked for ways of finding out – or had the opportunity to but wouldn't use them. I taught briefly in a girls' school and got really irritated by and jealous of the girls who simply wouldn't sing in assembly, many of them having beautiful voices; and the story told me by a friend of a boy she taught who had a beautiful, natural countertenor voice who, in her opinion, could have made a really good living with it but stopped singing completely because the other boys teased him about it. Just how many singers, male and female, do we lose in this way? I dread to think.

***

I moved to the Isle of Wight on Valentine's Day 2008. It was an uncharacteristically warm and sunny day and I took that to be a good omen for the future outcome, even though my two little cats were briefly traumatised by the journey. I started visiting the West Country again, an area of the UK I love but hadn't seen much of since my early twenties. My favourite county is Somerset (as is probably clear to anyone who's ever read anything I've written) and I stayed regularly in a lovely bungalow owned by Chris and Mike, who have now become friends. They no longer own it but I still stay in the same village as often as I can make the journey.

I'd driven over one Saturday afternoon for a week's break, listening to Classic FM on the car radio during the journey. Sibelius' *Finlandia* had been playing. I'm not that familiar with his work but what I know, I enjoy.

Unpacking my suitcase, I could hear someone singing 'Be Still My Soul' from the above-mentioned *Finlandia*. I couldn't locate the source of the sound, until I realised it was me. This sounds ridiculous, I know, but it doesn't make it any less true.

Apart from wandering round the bungalow in some sort of daze, going over and over the hymn until Chris and Mike (if they could hear me) must have become thoroughly sick of it, I don't really remember much about the hours following that breakthrough.

I knew who I was again.

Music has the power to reach the soul

Anoushka Shankar

GRANNIE LOUIE'S BIG ADVENTURE

Part 3: Jake

They were dropped off at exactly the same moment as she'd left.

'Oh do lighten up, Josie. If you don't enjoy my stories, I'll find someone who does and they can write them down for me. Maybe I can send them to some magazines and get a bit of extra cash in my purse.'

Josie was forced to back down in the face of opposition from Rick but mostly from Jake, who was adamant that Grannie Louie was 'fine. Mum. Just fine.'

***

But a lot had happened before they reached that point.

***

Jake was in awe of his new surroundings. He was sure he'd made the right choice. Freddie didn't need him anymore – probably never had, he was always closer to his mother – and Abi, well Abi found it hard to accept that after all these years he still had such a plethora of feelings about his Grannie. 'Let it go, love,' she'd say to him. You'll never know what happened to her now.' But he'd not been able to and Abi'd grown tired of his deliberations. They'd most likely be glad to see the back of him.

'These are your quarters,' Lindel told him. 'I hope they're to your liking. Please tell us if there is anything you lack.'

'Wow,' gasped Jake, not really believing the evidence of his own eyes. He saw a beautiful room that was all he'd ever dreamed of with a bed that folded up into the wall and a music console he could only describe as futuristic, where he could compose all the songs his brain and heart could conjure up. And, they'd already told him that he could do all the sports he wanted to. 'There'll be no-one here putting any limits on your activities. It's a learning environment, as well as a playground, where you can discover everything you'll ever want to know about yourself.' Hidrah was going to be easy to get on with and Jake was convinced he'd be happy.

***

'We have a real problem with this one,' said Lindel. 'We can't send them back unless they both go together; and they have to go willingly from their own choice.'

'Why do they need to go back? She's not his grandmother here. She's a pure soul, as is he,' replied Kaydock.

'He's not as advanced as we thought he was,' replied Lindel. 'He still feels bound to his other self, the one he had over there. He's suffering and we have no way of helping him.'

'He'll come through it.' Mithram was optimistic and didn't want to do anything hasty. 'We've had similar things before, where two members of the same bioclan came in fairly close succession in terms of their time. We just need to be vigilant.'

The meeting of the Council had gone on for a long time and in the end, the only decision they could make was to keep checking it out. Grannie Louie, at least, was

PART 3: JAKE

okay and surely, if anyone could guide Jake through it, it would be her.

***

'You're Grannie Louie!' he exclaimed. 'And who do you think I am? The Dog Poo Fairy?' He fell, rather than sat, into his armchair. Oh Hell! Could it be true? This was the woman he'd been fantasising about! All those things that kept flashing through his brain… Hell and Damnation! He'd learned how to filter his thoughts so the others couldn't read them but still, *he* knew they were there. He put his head in his hands. 'Oh good grief! I've got the hots for my own grandmother! Oh s***!'

How could it have happened? Now he knew, he could see the bright, intelligent eyes, full of curiosity and fun, the shape of the face and if he really thought about it, she wasn't that unlike the photos he'd seen of her when she was young. If you imagined her in all those old fashioned clothes, well, yes, he could definitely see it was her. 'OMG!' he wailed. 'What sort of perv is it who fancies his own gran?'

***

They'd been having the most wonderful time. Jake had even discovered that dancing wasn't quite the wussy thing he'd always thought it was. Far from it, it was every bit as athletic as, well, athletics, and you got to hold the girl. He especially liked that bit. He felt a pang sometimes. He couldn't forget how they'd all felt when Grannie Louie disappeared; and he'd like to tell Freddie how proud he was of him and how much he loved him. Things like that were so much easier here. No need for pretence. In fact, no hope of any, with everyone being able to tune into everyone else's thoughts and feelings. It sometimes felt as if they were one big, gloopy whole, these beings he was involved with here, but sometimes 'someone' popped out to remind themselves that they still had a 'me'.

He was enjoying the freedom that came with an unlimited body, in spite of the fact that it often felt that if he could do what he liked, achieve whatever he set out to just by thinking about it in the appropriate way, well, there was nothing to aspire to. It was all done for him and Jake liked to have a goal.

'You'll get used to it, Jake,' Grannie Louie promised him, 'and you'll find you love it. It's total freedom. No frustrations because our bodies simply won't do what we want them to. No dissatisfaction because none of us is more important or capable than anyone else. There's no competition and it leaves us free to discover the core of who we are and with it, unity with all the others.' Jake was restless, though. He wanted to prove himself and there'd be no chance here.

***

'I think you may have been right,' said Mithram. 'He's not settling down and his unease is causing disruption in the settlement.'

The result of the Council vote was unanimous. Trouble was, what would they say to Grannie Louie?

***

In the event, Grannie Louie was okay with it all. 'After all,' she told them, 'I'll be able to come back. My stay down

PART 3: JAKE

there won't even register here and it'll give all of them peace of mind.'

'He won't remember he was here,' said Lindel, 'but you will.'

'Oh, don't worry about that. I'll sort it out.'

***

And so it was – the deed was done and they were back in the granny flat, Josie looking angry and Rick wishing he could hide under a plant pot.

CONSULTATIONS PART 2

Elsewhere in Shortstoryland…
Another consulting room, another consultant, another client

Week 1

'Good morning. Please take a seat. My name is Max. Could you tell me in your own words what brings you here?'

'Hi Max. Nice to meet you. Thing is – I'm having difficulty in my marriage. It's not working and I think it's time to throw in the towel but well, you can't just turn your back on twenty two years, can you?'

'Could you give me a little more information about what is going on for you?'

'Well, he only wants me for sex. And he uses those bloody blue pills all the time. How many marriages have they caused to break up? Are there any figures, Do – Max?'

'I'm less interested in the figures than in how this is affecting your life. Can you tell me something about that?'

'It's like having a broom handle shoved up you. It's horrible. And it's offensive. He should want me for me, not because he's got some pills from the chemist. Do you know what they cost, Doctor? Enough for a week's groceries now there are just the two of us, that's what. And then, the other night, or rather morning, he woke me up out of the blue, said he didn't need a pill and how about it.'

Silence. The client picks at her fingernails.

'Okay. And how did this make you feel?'

'Bloody annoyed. I had an important assembly in the morning and I told him that over dinner – which, incidentally, I always have to cook. No equal opportunities in our house – but all he wanted to talk about was how tired he is all the time because he can't sleep. No-one in the neighbourhood can sleep, I would imagine, what with the shed door banging all night. And I didn't want to be bothered with all that, not in the middle of the night.'

'So, forgive me if I'm stating the obvious but I'm picking up that you were not pleased with this approach at what was, for you, an inappropriate time. Is that right?'

'Yes.'

'So could you tell me how you responded?'

'Like any woman would. I told him what to do with his bits and went and slept in the spare room. The assembly went really well, by the way.'

'I'm pleased to hear that. So, did either of you approach the subject to see if you could find a way of avoiding this sort of incident in the future?'

'No. I went out with some friends that evening to see that new film about the dog. You know the one I mean, Do – Max? Oh, what a shame. Anyway, it's really good, so if it's on in a cinema round your way, I'd go and see it if I were you. I left him a sandwich. He likes ham and tomato, so I made him a couple. And a piece of the iced sponge he enjoys. Made sure he had all his favourites. I didn't want him to go hungry.'

'Did you find going to the film helped in any way?'

'A bit, yes. It's good to be with people who know you, care about you –

The client stares ahead at the floor, thinking deeply. She looks up at the consultant and gives him a half-smile.

-people who understand you. But when I got home he was sitting in the armchair snoring with the television blaring away to itself, and I thought, well, this is someone who can't sleep and never talks about anything else, and there he is making enough noise to wake Australia. He never wants to go out. Never wants to do anything at all, except for sit in the chair, bang on about his work and his insomnia and bother me with his unreasonable sexual "needs" as he describes them. I thought all that was over long ago and I can't say I ever missed it.'

'Okay. It seems to me that there are various strands to this issue: you would like to go out and do things with him, you would like to talk more meaningfully about the things that bother you, such as your work; you'd like there to be more equality in the way the household chores are arranged. But my impression is that underlying all this is the single issue – and correct me if I'm wrong – that you are either unable or unwilling to speak to each other about the things that are troubling you.'

'Oh, he can talk alright Do – Max. He can tell me about his terminally dull job, his secretary – I thought he might be having an affair with her at one time, but no such luck –

And what would be the outcome if he had, I wonder

– his sleepless nights, but if I try to do the same, it's "I'm off to bed now to see if I can get some sleep". It's one rule for him and one for me.'

'Would I be right in thinking that if you approach this at all, it happens late at night, after the household matters have been settled and you are both tired?'

'Yeah. It's when we're both relaxed, so it seems like the best time. Only we don't even bother to do that now, because it just ends up in a row or him suggesting we smooth it all over with him taking one of the pills.'

Indeed, the ubiquitous blue pills aren't quite the panacea we've been led to believe, are they. This must be the second time this month I've heard this from a female client and it's only the ninth. 'And you don't think that this is a suitable solution.'

'Course I don't. I've just told you that.'

'I can see how you would feel that there might be other ways of responding to these challenges. Is there anything you can suggest yourself that you think might help?'

CONSULTATIONS

'Well, if he'd listen to me sometimes. That'd help. But when he does, he just finds solutions like, for instance, a couple of weeks ago, Warren, that's our eldest, was having problems at uni. He said so on the phone and told me all about it, so I told Bill and he started coming up with all the answers, the Problem Solving Approach we call it at school, but sometimes you don't need answers. Sometimes all you need is to get it out of your system. And anyway, it wasn't our problem to solve and I don't think we should interfere, even though I want to. All the time. I hate seeing the boys unhappy. He does, too, only he won't admit it. Thinks it makes him look weak. Only I've tried to explain that it's natural to worry about your kids. He won't have it though. 'They're adults now,' he says. But I know he worries as much as I do. I only wanted him to listen to me, not to put the entire world right in one conversation.'

'Okay. I'm afraid we're coming to the end of our time together today. For 'homework', could I ask that in the coming week, you choose a television programme that you would both be interested in and that when it is finished, you talk about it. Ask him if he enjoyed it, which bit he liked most. That type of thing. Leave the big issues alone for the time being. How does that sound?

'Well, I can't see a lot of point really. I mean, it's not the television that causes the problems.'

'I see that, but it might be better to take things slowly, try to establish lines of communication in a neutral fashion first.'

'All right then. If you think it's worth it, I'll give it a try. See you next week.'

Week 2

The client walks in with a face like thunder, throws herself in the chair and glares at Max.

'I realised when I left last week, you think this is all down to me. You don't think I listen to him enough, do you.'

Good morning to you, too. 'I'm sorry you feel like that. That is not my intention and certainly not my interpretation of your difficulties. Maybe my explanation was inadequate – I was hoping that if we found neutral ground where you could start talking to each other, in good time it would make it possible to approach the bigger issues.'

'Oh. Well I tried, only he asked me why I was giving him the inquisition over a film when I never bother to ask him about his work. So I said he never asks me about mine, either, and he said it was different, because his is important and he doesn't get twelve weeks holiday a year so we ended up having another row.'

'May I ask, does your husband know that you are coming to see me?'

'Course not. It'd just be something else he could charge me with, as well as going out with the girls, spending too much time preparing lessons, not bothering with the garden because "after all, I finish work at 4 in the afternoon and have most of the year off in holiday, and it doesn't look after itself." It was him that wanted a big garden, Do – Max, and he won't let me get anyone to do it. What do I know about gardening? Nothing, that's what, and what's more, I don't WANT to know. "It's a waste of money getting a gardener, when we're both still young and fit," he says. And then he starts banging on about how he can't sleep and he's tired and will I just leave him in peace. And he STILL hasn't done the shed door. The neighbours are complaining now, and who can blame them? –

Maybe I should get the shed door in for an opinion. It sounds like it might be the most rational member of the household.

I'm going to get a man in to do it and if he doesn't like it, it's tough. I'm going to leave him anyway.'

'This seems to be a bit of a sudden decision. Would you like to talk it through?'

'What's to talk through? He wants all the sympathy and understanding from me but won't give me any in return. He expects everything on his terms. He doesn't support me at all, not with anything; not with the home, not with the boys and not with my career. Just says if it's giving me grief, I should give it up and stay at home. He says I could get the garden in order then and that would help us both.'

'As you pointed out in our last session, turning your back on twenty two years is not a straightforward strategy. Has anything specific happened to trigger this decision?'

The client looks distracted, plays with her fingernails and looks over the doctor's shoulder through the window

'He got home from work one night and said Janice – that's his secretary – had made a complaint about him because he'd snapped at her. He was upset enough about that but never gets upset about what's happening between us. Just watches the cricket and wildlife programmes. Said he was in trouble, so I said well now you're in trouble here, too, because I'm leaving you.'

The client, clearly exhausted, pauses for breath. She looks down at her hands and rubs her nose. Distracted, she looks round the room as if trying to find comfort in the furnishings. Max lets her gather her thoughts.

'How did you feel after telling him you were leaving him?'

'Dreadful. Absolutely bloody dreadful.'

'Are you totally sure this is the path you wish to pursue?'

The client bursts into tears. Max hands her a box of tissues and allows her to cry herself out.

'No doctor. No, it's not. I want to mend it all and make it work.'

'Shall we see if we can find ways that might help you to do so?'

'Please doctor. Yes please.'

THE VAN

1
The Woman

Another day. Another first day of the rest of my life. Bright. Crisp. The sun's gorgeous, glinting off the waves, even though that van's obstructing the view. Time for my first coffee of the morning. Can't hang around like this forever.

What's on today? Ah good. Nothing but a meeting with Lucy over lunch. 'Lucinda Carrington-Critchley.' You'd never guess she was that sweet little thing if you knew nothing of her but her name. Lovely woman. Warm, gentle. I wonder how she sees herself? Lucy or Lucinda Carrington-Critchley? Maybe I should ask. Maybe not. A bit rude, possibly. What's in a name? Quite a lot if you think about it.

Right. Focus. Fill the kettle. Put it on the stand. Switch on. Now, count the breaths, one, two, three – gosh, this mindfulness business is hard work. What do I do now? Listen to the birds or concentrate on the breathing? I don't remember everyday living being this complicated before. Pour the water on the coffee, freshly ground, of course. Take the toast out of the toaster. Butter it. I don't know about this 'living in the moment' being good for you. It's driving me doolally. I'm taking this next door and having breakfast on the sofa.

That van ruins it. The neighbours don't bother to complain anymore. No point, really. He won't move it. What does he do in there all day? No-one ever sees him. I suppose he goes to all-night supermarkets to get his provisions. I thought he might be dead at one point. He wasn't, though. You hear his radio sometimes, and his footsteps banging around on the floor.

***

Ah, that's better. Clean and clothed. Can you do the ironing mindfully? Of course you can. I don't think I'll bother, though. There's an interesting programme on 4Extra. Much more fun than counting the number of times the iron skims across the jeans. Lucy's not coming 'til 1, so there's plenty of time to prepare. It's only an assortment of salads anyway. I've got to tell her I can't be involved anymore. It's gone on for too long and it's unfair to her. Trouble is, she's not the sort of person you want to let down. Not a single bad cell in her whole body. How many cells are there in a body do you suppose? It might say on the internet. Put a reminder on the fridge magnet to look it up. Mind you, Lucy's four foot ten – or should that be a hundred and forty five centimetres? – weighing forty one kilos. She's bound to have fewer cells than a giant like me. Or have we got the same number and mine are bigger than hers? I wonder what she thinks of the van. She's never mentioned it. She probably thinks it's mine.

***

It must feel like being in prison, spending your entire life in a van. Unless he goes walking at night, when no-one can see him. Alan Bennett had that woman parked on his driveway for years. I wonder what he really thought

THE VAN

about it. Perhaps I'll write and ask him. At least that van's in the road.

Maybe we should set up one of those camera trap thingies and see if anything happens during the hours of darkness when he thinks no-one can see him. There are some lovely walks round here. It could be quite spooky at night. Or maybe the moonlight makes it magical.

It's three years now. Imagine that. Three years in a van. It's sparkling clean. I bet he's house proud with everything glowing and in its place. What does he wear? Pyjamas probably. If you never leave a van, you don't need evening dress, do you. Has he worn the same pair for the entire time?

Time to stop ruminating about that wretched van and go out the back and do a bit of weeding! Pity the gardener has to do the front. It was a good idea to have it planted up with a succession of bulbs, so there's all year colour with minimum input. It does look nice. Even with the van right in front of the window.

***

It's times like this when you could do with a man around the house, what with the skirting boards being chipped and the wallpaper starting to peel. Home improvements were never my thing. Since he moved out, it just doesn't get done. Funny the things we miss about people. Some people miss the companionship but me, well, I miss having an odd job man. It took eons to find someone to sort the socket out in the bathroom and it cost a small fortune! Still, I guess that's what you have to accept if you're going it alone.

***

Ah yes, nothing better than a nice cup of tea. Darjeeling. 'The champagne of teas', that's what it says on the box.

People ask me why we broke up and honestly, there's no tangible reason. It'd just started to feel as if there was more to being alive than what we were doing. There were no cross words. Maybe that was the trouble. Some people say if you don't argue, you don't care. Well, that's certainly possible in this case.

***

Why is that van getting on my nerves so today? It's been there three whole years now and until recently, I'd hardly

THE VAN

noticed it. Not unless the neighbours complained. It really is an eyesore. What does anyone get from living in a van in front of the house?

Let's get going on the lunch and forget about the wretched van.

Ah. Now I see it. Exactly three years today. That's when the Absolute came through, only he said he'd never accept it. Well, he's proved his point, I suppose. He's lived in that bloody van every single day since.

Trouble is, every minute the van's out there, I'm incarcerated here in the kitchen. It might have been better to stay married.

A BOX OF MASKS

She'd read somewhere that some clever bloke believed that life is a box of masks. Apparently, we change our mask according to who we're with. 'Is that really true?' she asked herself. 'Isn't it just that individual people see us through the lens that brings their own view of the world into focus?'

She got on with clearing the sink. How did it get so filthy? 'Black tea, I guess. It stains everything. Imagine what it does to your insides.' The scouring pad was falling apart. 'Another trip to the supermarket,' she told herself, a jaded tone creeping into her voice. Trouble was, it closed at six and it was still light then. She'd preferred not to be seen in public. She'd have to find out about internet shopping. It was all the rage these days.

Waiting for the kettle to boil – another cup of black tea, another load of tannin coating the inside of the china; another scouring pad? She pondered again on the idea of being someone different for everyone she met. 'Exhausting. Totally exhausting. But then I don't meet many people, so how would I know?'

The tea was bitter and far too strong. It made her tongue feel sore and her throat dry. 'If anyone saw me now, they'd think I was wearing my "Life is yuck" mask, because that's what this horrible tea's making me look like and more to the point, feel. Surely we're who we are in the moment, not an alternative version of ourselves that we dig out for each different person we encounter. I mean, how would you remember?'

It was way too complicated. Like that thing she'd read in the magazine on *Multiple Personality Disorder*. 'Is that what actors have?' she wondered. Probably not. They create characters from someone else's words and leave them behind in the theatre. She knew that because she'd heard them say so on *Woman's Hour*. Still, it must be fatiguing to adopt another new personality day after day, week after week; confusing at the very least.

She looked at the clock. Not long now. She'd have another go at getting those disgusting mugs clean again. She'd heard that denture cleaner did the trick, so she'd better add that to the list for PriceSlashers. What picture would she present to the world if anyone saw her now? House proud? Meticulous and keen to impress? She laughed. Nothing could be further from the truth.

She glanced again at the clock. Ah yes. It was exactly the right moment to get going. She put on her cloak, got the mask – this time she chose the black one with red circles painted round the eye holes – picked up the knife and went out into the night to do her worst.

THE VAN

2
The neighbour

I see her sometimes in the garden. She seems so happy, particularly when the gardener's here. Mind you, what can you expect? All tanned torso and rippling muscles. She's put a bit of weight on recently but she never goes out, so bound to spread a bit, I suppose, even if you watch what you're eating.

Derek – that's my husband – he says we should leave her to it, and Ollie – my son – well, I don't think he even bothers to form an opinion. Why should he?

Her groceries arrive on the same van as mine. He has to bring the bags down the side of hers though. She won't let anyone in through the front door. Nice bloke, the delivery guy. We had a woman delivering them during the lockdowns – I wonder what happened to her – but there's been a long succession of drivers since. Don't you think they do a wonderful job, these delivery guys? And thank goodness they do, because she'd never get any provisions if they didn't.

The girls don't visit her anymore. Pity. They're nice, both of them. One of them – can't remember which – has a couple of kids herself. Fancy never seeing your own grandchildren.

I've suggested she gets the gardener (Jim, I think he said his name was), to put a gate in between her garden and mine, then she could come round for tea sometimes and

THE VAN

I could go round there. No need to go indoors. We've got a summerhouse here. Derek built it when Ollie was small, so he could have his own special place. Derek wanted more but I wasn't going through all that again. They say you forget the pain of childbirth but I know I never have. Put me off everything if you see what I mean. I think Derek probably went elsewhere in the end but I never minded. I wasn't that interested in the first place, if you want to know the truth. I agree with that Shirley Valentine woman. Like shopping. A lot of pushing and shoving and you come out with nothing much worth having anyway. Except I got Ollie, so I can't complain.

Poor Derek.

Ollie's at university now. Edinburgh. His last year of Psychology and Philosophy. I'm hoping he'll come back when he's finished but Derek says I'm being stupid. He only comes back at Christmas but that's because Edinburgh's such a long way away. He doesn't talk much when I phone him. He tells me a bit about the course and how he's doing but nothing else. I wonder if he's got a girl. Or a boy. And if he ever thinks about his mum.

Derek's right. It is a real eyesore but from here, we can more or less ignore it. It doesn't obscure the view of the sea and the cliffs and it's nice to see the birds landing on top. Occasionally you hear his radio and sometimes his footsteps are as clear as anything. Not much space for a walk in a van that size, so goodness only knows what he's doing. I wonder he doesn't ask our delivery people to sort him out at the same time. Maybe he favours a different supermarket.

Here comes the gardener. I wonder what he's doing this week. Three hours, he's out there, rain or shine. Where does she get the money from? She says she works from home but nobody seems to know what she does. If you ask her, she's sort of evasive. 'Oh this and that,' she'll say. 'This and that what?' I want to ask but never do. She's not the sort of person you would ask, even if she weren't living like a hermit. I never found out what he did for a living, either, but I can't imagine he still does it now he's living in the van. Derek's an accountant and they've got a reputation for being dull. Well, sometimes stereotypes are accurate, aren't they.

I always had a crush on him, you know. He only cared about her though. By all accounts, from appearances it seems he still does.

There they go, laughing and joking. He's supposed to be doing the weeding and pruning, not flirting! He puts his arm round her sometimes and I saw him kiss her neck once. What's she got? Well, I guess you can say she's got a doting husband and this gardener, and he could win the odd beauty contest or two. So yes. She's got them alright. Not that I'm jealous. I've got Derek.

I wonder what her girls think. A mother who never sets foot outside the house and a father living in a van on the road outside. Their friends and in-laws must think they've stepped out of a futuristic novel, where people don't interact anymore because there's all this Zoom nonsense and Facebook and Twitter. No need to spend time with people if you can do it all over the net. Far fewer opportunities for rows, I suppose.

Derek and I don't bother to row anymore. No point. They never used to row next door, not once in all the years they lived there and you can hear in these houses if it all kicks off. Maybe they should have done.

Sometimes, when Derek's out with his snooker friends for the weekend and I know she's in bed – you can tell, because the light's on in the back – I go round to the van and we sit and have a chat. Sometimes a bit more than a chat. Sometimes I'd like it to be a *lot* more than a chat but life's complicated enough and heaven only knows what it'd do to her if she found out. I don't want anything on my conscience. And Derek's always been good to me, so I wouldn't want to hurt him, either.

Can you be jealous of a woman who commits herself to solitary confinement in her own home? Of course you can't. What a ridiculous thought.

Derek's what they used to call a Man's Man. The Man in the Van – that's what Derek and I call him – he's not a Man's Man. He's sort of sweet and kind. Still, she obviously didn't think so. They say you never know someone 'til you live with them, so maybe we've misjudged him. He's so concerned, though. He thinks she might be losing a few marbles because of the isolation. I wonder how he can tell when he spends all his time in the van.

Good grief! The gardener's going into the house! Surely they're not going – no, she's staying in the garden. She's got a sandwich and a can of something. Maybe he needs to use the facilities. Even gardeners have to answer the call, don't they. I've never seen it happen before, in spite of the number of times he's been here. I'll keep an eye on it. After all, if there's something going off that shouldn't be, he needs to know. I mean, I know they're divorced and all that but I wouldn't want to see him made a fool of.

Derek's going straight off with his snooker friends tonight, so I'll be here on my own. I can't go round to see her, not unless we see each other in the garden. Maybe I'll go and knock on the door of the van. I'll call Curl up and Dye in the morning, see if they can sort my hair out.

Not for anything special, you understand, just because it'd be nice to have a change. Smarten myself up a bit. Make myself feel attractive again.

The question is: 'who for?'

FREYA'S OUTRAGE

Freya realised it was time to step out of her comfort zone. 'Time to do something outrageous,' she decided. But what? 'This is the twenty first century,' she mused. 'Outrageous is the new normal.'

Wandering around the Mall on her shopping trip, she acted on a whim – 'The longest journey starts with a single step,' she thought. 'When did I last treat myself to a drink out?' Unable to remember, she postponed the usual round of shops and purchases and stopped off in the first coffee shop she came to, a rather grandiose place for all its diminutive size, and asked for the richest, sickliest beverage they could create. It was thus that she found herself enjoying a full milk latte with maple syrup and whipped cream with chocolate sprinkles to spruce it up a bit, give it a bit of bite. 'A bit over the top for a coffee, perhaps, but a worthy start to my quest.'

Settling down at her desk to do some work – her neighbour's book-keeping, as dull a job as you could ever imagine – she started to contemplate a new way of making her living. Something with a bit of oomph, something that might raise the odd eyebrow if she had to tell someone about it at a party. Not that she was ever invited to any, of course. 'Being a Certified Book-keeper isn't really a job designed to bring out the glamourous side of a person,' she thought. 'Still, it'll stand me in good stead when I branch out into my new career, whatever that's going to be.'

Luxuriating in the bath, she came up with the perfect plan, and it was in this wise that Twilight Time was born, Escorts for the Discerning Woman of Mature Vintage. 'Not a great deal of escorting going on, maybe, but providing a service leading to a lot of satisfaction in a decidedly unsatisfactory world, and more exciting than sorting out other people's financial headaches,' she thought.

Sometime later, sinking back into her armchair one evening, Freya realised that this outrageous way of life she'd created for herself was her new normal and for that reason, no longer fulfilling its brief. 'Back to the drawing board,' she decided.

What would she come up with next?

THE VAN

3
The man

It's not that bad, you know. It's not really a van. It's more of one of those homes on wheels. Candy always hated them but she's an impatient driver, always was. There's plenty of space and I don't need much. The girls think I'm mad and it's too cramped but it serves its purpose. I don't see them much these days. They won't come here. They don't even go to see Candy anymore and if they phone, she's always going on about Lucy. Lucinda Corringshit Carbide or some such. (Where do they get these names from?) They don't know her and get bored hearing stories about someone they've never laid eyes on. Luna's six now and Esme three and a half. She's missing out on her grandchildren's childhoods. Poor Candy.

Candy, Or Cath. That's Catherine Anna Diane York. And before you ask, yes, she's definitely good enough to eat.

We're always being told that men don't talk but that's not always our fault. If we have a go, it's 'have you sorted out the u-bend yet?' or 'there's a dead bird in the garden. You know I hate dead birds. Why haven't you got rid of it?' If they want to talk – now that's a different matter. Then, it's warbling on like a black cap forced into celibacy and set free for the first time in years; and it's all 'oh, I know you men aren't interested in talking. Go off down the pub then and watch the bloody football. You're doing no good here.' So we give up trying.

This thing with Candy. I'd love to talk about it. It'd be great to talk to her. Find out how she's doing, if she's coping, because quite frankly, it doesn't look to me as if she is.

Sarah, the woman from next door, she comes round sometimes. Always really late and only if there's no moon to speak of. Gave me a terrible shock the first time I heard the scratching at the door. I wonder what Candy thinks of that but she probably doesn't tell her. She brings me food sometimes. Now, that I don't object to. It's good to get a bit of decent home cooking from time to time and she can certainly rustle up a treat. She brought a magazine round once with stories about cosmetic surgery that went wrong. Wanted to know if I thought she needed any! Frankly, I've never even bothered to look at her properly so what she should do with her face is entirely her own affair.

I had a nose job once. It was really painful but worth it. I had a hooter the size of a fog horn so it made a massive difference to how I looked. Maybe I should tell Sarah that. It might help her decide. But the point is, while she was flicking through it, I noticed one of Candy's stories. She writes under the name of Melissa Hurst and used to earn a really good living at it. I hope she still does. I asked if I could have a look at the magazine, pretending I was interested in going under the knife but I had a look and bloody hell! That story was dark. I mean, really dark. All about how sensuous it is to cut up meat and comparing chicken with beef. Candy was a vegetarian, so I can't imagine how she knows. Unless her diet's changed. It'd explain why she's got so porky. Mind you, she was like a stick insect before, so it's good to see her with a few curves. She doesn't drive now. Never leaves the house, only to go in the back garden. I see her a lot looking out of the window, peering at the van, looking longingly at the sea and the cliffs. Poor Candy.

THE VAN

I've been trying to find out who this Lucinda is. It looks like she's the only real contact Cath has with the outside world. She can't be local. No-one's heard of her. I hope she's helping Cath with everything. I'd rather be stuck here in the van than incarcerated in that house, no matter how lovely it is. I can't imagine she's doing much with the upkeep. Equality seems to have fallen short at the point where women do their own DIY. At least, it did in our house. Mustn't generalise. It's probably not like that everywhere and the young ones are probably different. Chloe – she's our youngest – does all her own, I know, but Chloe's shacked up with Belle and they're both broke, so I guess they've had to learn.

I used to be the manager in a big supermarket but got fed up with it, so once the divorce came through I gave it the old heave-ho and never looked back. I've got a better life now, in spite of not having Candy and living in a van. I go to the all night gym and there's a café there where I get hot food. I'm a lot healthier than I was, and not being stuck in a shop all day listening to the customers and staff complaining about this and that or making decisions about where and how the baked beans should be stacked – well, would you miss it? It did me a favour in that respect, when she decided she'd had enough of married bliss, only I didn't realise it then of course.

Sarah told me the other day the gardener had been into the house. Nosey old cow. Still, I like her coming here. It means I get to know more about what Cath's up to and if she seems alright. She asked me if I didn't think I might be just a 'teeny bit obsessed' with my ex-wife and if it was healthy. I don't honestly think I care.

When she lost her job – redundancy, last in first out and she was the last in by a very long mile – it knocked her confidence. I thought she'd get over it but she didn't, not really. She did great with hiding it but if you live with someone, you know if they're not quite up to par. She reinvented herself as a writer and it was great. She got a lot of her self-esteem back and earned loads of dosh. More than I did at the supermarket. It gave her the chance to spread her wings but she couldn't face people. Said she was ashamed that she'd been given the boot, even though it wasn't her fault and she was doing so well with the writing. Her stories were never that dark though. Something's really exploded in her brain. Come to think of it, the meat story was narrated by Lucy. Blimey.

But it's okay. I get to chat to her once a week. The voice could have been a problem but that's been solved by adopting a Brummie accent; and the nose job's made me unrecognisable. I love doing the garden. It was supposed to be fifteen quid an hour and she only wanted an hour a week, but the way it's developed, what with her wanting so much done out there and enjoying a good chat, it's ended up being a fiver an hour.

Thing is, if I manage to win her back, will I need to tell her who I really am? I suppose the real give away will be getting rid of the van.

DEFINITELY NOT BUNTHORNE'S BRIDE

Right then. Iolanthe told me that you won't know who I am so I'll fill you in. I'm Patience, the principle female character in the opera of the same name. A milk maid. Sweet seventeen and never been kissed. At least Mr Gilbert didn't make us all aristocrats and posh people. You have to give him that. We women are all supposed to be fawning after the terminally tiresome Bunthorne, who spends his time writing doggerel – seriously, I'm not exaggerating. It's genuinely dreadful – because the aesthetic movement was big at the time and they wanted to send it up. Thing is, in spite of all the brilliant political satire and subtlety of the texts, at the bottom line they're still about women desperate to find a man and men who can't – or rather, this being the late nineteenth century – don't want to keep it in their pants but are required to in the event of a vaguely attractive woman showing up on the scene. And then, of course, there's the Elderly Woman, usually given lovely music (credit where it's due and Mr Sullivan deserves that) who's spent her life unable to find a man, probably because she's had to care for assorted elderly relatives without any help and who has to take whoever's on offer if she wants a relationship in her sunset years. At least she always finds someone. In truth, we all need love.

So that was me at the beginning of the action, perfectly happy in my life of milk-maiding, and all of a sudden, this Bunthorne oaf bursts onto the scene, panting around me and making me feel quite nauseous, if not actually threatened.

It's a good job, you know. An honest living: out in the country, not stuck in the city all day, where you can get breathing disorders because of all the air pollution. And it's indoors, so there's no danger of a suntan. I got one once and as it wore off, it really itched. I won't do that again. But it's a really good job for someone like me, because it's not intellectually demanding, so I can think of serious things, like how to make the best of my natural attributes and how fortunate I am not being able to get to shops and be tempted by assorted chocolate treats, spoiling my figure and giving me spots.

Right. Now you know about my work, let me tell you a bit about myself. I'm rather gorgeous, even though I know it's not really right for me to say so but truly, if that's the way it is, I simply have to be honest. Would you really want me to lie? I'm dainty, with an hourglass figure and the teeniest of waists, with lovely golden curls and eyes like lapis lazuli. My smile, so they tell me, can turn a bar of dairy milk into a chocolate fountain at fifty paces. And of course, I have one of those delicate, tinkly voices that hits the high notes with no effort at all, just floats off on the wind. What's not to admire? I suppose being worshipped by all those men is the price I have to pay. Never mind.

I'll tell you a secret though. I've never, ever, not once in my whole life ever been in love. What's the point? You start off billing and cooing, eyes only for each other, every available minute spent either being in their company or dreaming of how wonderful it'll be when you are and then before you know it, it's 'I cleared up the dog shit yesterday. It's your turn today' and 'What's so bloody difficult about putting the bloody toilet lid down?' The next step's dividing up the CD collection and arguing over who gets the Paddington Bear bed linen. Truly, you *can* learn from other people's mistakes.

They paired me off with the diabolically dull Grosvenor at the end. Pretended he was my childhood sweetheart. Heaven forbid. Not quite as bad as Bunthorne but who could be? The man could do with a good wash for a start, a decent square meal and a proper haircut wouldn't come amiss, either. Dreadlocks look lovely on the right people but Bunthorne? I think not. It was really Saphir I wanted to pair up with but I never got consulted. It wouldn't have done back in those days, I suppose. Queen Victoria would have hated it. But then, as my old mother used to say, it wouldn't have been Queen Vic getting it.

Big G was okay. He didn't bother me much, if you get my drift. Too busy dreaming about long walks in the hills and going off to The Smoke to see what was going on in the fashion world. He looks after himself, he really does. He engages in a lot of sport, running and wild swimming and that type of thing. Nothing that would risk spoiling his perfect body and face, like rugby or boxing. I don't ask him much about himself really. Never been that bothered. He was foisted on me, so why should I be interested? But he spends a lot of time making sure he's well preserved – I think that's the right phrase – and in the peak of health.

I was always a bit of a career woman. Never wanted all that home and babies stuff, so I told Big G I suffer from headaches for three weeks of the month and when that abates a bit, I get women's problems. Well, that sorted that side of things out.

He has this tendency to flop about the place, all arms and legs and them getting in the way all the time, so you trip over them. He can't help it, not really. It's his genes, I suppose. And well, to be fair – and I ALWAYS like to be fair – they thrust me upon him, just like he was thrust on me. Not literally, of course. Nothing like that. But it accounts for his lack of interest in me. Very odd though. No man has ever found me resistible before.

So anyway, I kept my head down, worked hard and flirted when Big G wasn't there to see, ending up getting myself promoted. I saved up REALLY hard and in the end, I bought the farm. It's been converted into a wildflower meadow and nature reserve with a Visitor Centre and Café and now I'm absolutely rolling in it, you know. Cash, that it, not cow dung. Saphir does the accounts. She's good with figures, both numerical and mine.

Big G's gone off with Bunthorne and I believe they're living in a bothy somewhere in the Hebrides. Good for them. I do like a happy ending.

What was it that other chap said? All's well that ends well. I'll second that.

2015

'This is definitely *not* what I burned my bra for.' Laura was again baby-sitting the grandchildren while their mother was on a night shift. 'It seems to me that all that campaigning we did for "Women's Liberation" has, in many ways, made a woman's lot even worse.'

Getting them to bed that evening had been even more harrowing than the traditional nightmare and had left her exhausted. Resisting the temptation for a glass of wine before turning in herself, she'd settled for a mug of drinking chocolate; and very comforting it was, too.

She joined the WLM when everything had been signed and sealed after John's death. What a time that had been. He'd realised there was something wrong with the tea before even lifting the cup to his mouth. 'So,' he'd said, his face contorted with rage, 'what's going on. Are you trying to drug me or poison me? Is that it?'

She'd been terrified but had managed to convince him – she hoped – that whatever was wrong with the tea had been an accident and her shocked reaction had been horror that she could make such a terrible mistake.

'First thing tomorrow, I'm phoning Dr Anderson. You're going back into that hospital.' With that, he picked up his coat and banged out of the house.

When she answered the door after a sleepless night, convinced that he'd gone to the hospital about her or far worse, the police station, she was horrified to see two young officers on the doorstep.

'Mrs Garvey?' enquired the woman.

'That's me, yes. What can I do for you?' she replied.

'May we come in?' The police woman looked concerned, caring, and Laura was sure they'd come to tell her the ambulance was on its way and she was returning to the ward.

The three of them went into the lounge and Laura offered them a cup of tea.

'No thanks,' said the man, prompting her to believe that they were worried she might want to poison them, too.

'I'm afraid we have some rather shocking and sad news,' said the woman. 'Your husband, John, left the Crown Inn last night having had far too much to drink. He walked straight out onto the road into the path of an oncoming car. There was nothing that could be done for him. Several witnesses were at the scene, all of whom vouched that the driver could have done nothing to avoid him.'

Laura was so relieved, she laughed. The two young officers looked at each other, aware that shock hits people in different ways and the reality of the situation hadn't yet struck home.

'Is there anyone we can contact to be with you?' asked the man.

'No,' she said. 'No, but please let me make you a drink.'

'If you tell me where the kitchen is, I'll go and do it,' he said.

'No,' replied Laura, a little too fiercely, but if they noticed, they didn't let it register. 'I think it'd be better if I did something.'

And so it was that Laura found herself a widow owning a very nice house and having quite a considerable sum of money at her disposal at the age of twenty five. John had been a banker, was significantly older than she was and had made many shrewd investments. What he'd not done, though, was make a will, so everything he had was now hers.

Before she got married, she'd never really understood why people joined things like the Women's Liberation Movement. There'd been no reason to question her place in life, nothing to make her think that there could be any better way than the traditional route she'd been trained for – marriage, home-making, children – and whilst she'd found the first two of these three decidedly unsatisfying, she had no reason to believe that motherhood wouldn't be the salvation she was hoping for. But now John was gone and she was independent, why, she wanted to make the best of it.

There'd been rather more examining each other's vulvas than she'd bargained for, but they'd encouraged her to question, to get A' levels, go to university – she'd got a good degree in chemistry – and found part-time work in a laboratory studying air quality. This direction was infinitely more fulfilling than the one she'd been brought up to believe was her only destiny. In spite of everything, she knew she owed a lot of it to John, who'd taught her far more than she wanted to acknowledge.

Laura made her daughter breakfast – cheese on toast and builder's tea – when she got back off shift ready to take the children to school. Her son-in-law refused to do it, just like he refused to have the kids all night when Jilly was working. 'You don't need to work. Give it up,' he kept telling her. But she wouldn't and he made it clear that if she worked, she'd have to 'take the consequences.' The consequences were that her work as a paramedic, although theoretically part-time, meant that arranging childcare was hell. She knew her mother was too old to be expected to look after a lively boy and girl of seven and eight but what else could she do? She didn't earn enough to pay anyone; and who would be available to work around her shift pattern anyway? If she was honest, having come to motherhood late – very late – she often felt she was a bit too old herself but wouldn't be without them. Adam was adamant that there'd be no help from him, either practically or financially and his only contribution to the home was the mortgage – to be paid off in the very near future, so even that would be stopping soon – and his half of the household bills. She'd wanted the kids, so she'd have to provide for them; and she wanted to work, she'd have to make her own arrangements.

***

'Just how many pills do you take?' asked her mother.

'There are for depression, this one's for my blood pressure, this one's to stop me getting migraine and this one's a multi-vitamin.'

'Aren't there other ways of sorting these things out? Yoga or tai chi or something?' Laura wanted to know.

'Are you joking, mum? Have you seen my schedule?'

'But surely you could fit something in. And the multi-vitamins – I thought I'd taught you about nutrition and healthy eating when you were little,' said Laura.

2015

'No time for this now mum. Thanks for having the kids again and getting them ready for school. See you tomorrow.'

Nope. Women's Liberation didn't seem to have helped much at all.

Laura met Tom at a conference in Birmingham and they'd hit it off immediately. She was determined never to marry again but he'd moved in with her after six months. After all, cohabiting was okay these days. No-one expected you to have the certificate and the ring anymore. She wouldn't have a joint bank account or let him put any money into the house, wouldn't let him do anything to it and wouldn't take gifts from him unless they cost beneath a very low threshold. She was never going to be dependent on a man again. The only thing she permitted was a contribution to the cost of raising Jilly and hiring an au pair. He did his best to make it up to her in other ways: taking her out as often as he could, participating fully in Jilly's upbringing and the smooth functioning of the house, encouraging them both to live life to its absolute limits. They'd been truly happy until he had a heart attack at work two weeks before he was due to retire. She'd loved and respected him; and not once had she been tempted to murder him.

Back in her own home after a gruelling day at work, Jilly was at the end of her tether. 'My job is important to me. And they're YOUR children, too. Would it really be too much to come to the parents' evening?'

'I'm tired when I get back from work. I just want to relax. You'll have to go alone,' he'd said.

'I get tired, too. I work hard, do all the housework because I can't afford a cleaner, have to do all the childcare because you won't contribute anything so I can pay for an au pair or child minder and you expect everything to be spic and span with the dinner on the table when you get in. If that's not enough, you expect me to entertain your friends and business associates,' she said.

'You know the answer to that. Give up that job. You earn next to nothing and you're only a glorified taxi driver.

Winded by this, when Jilly finally found the wherewithal to answer, he simply cut her off.

'Subject's closed,' he'd said, and went off for an evening's relaxation at the pub. Jilly wondered if she could increase the anti-depressants, because the dose she was on at the moment definitely wasn't doing the trick.

Laura's house was big enough, no doubt about that and it was certainly easier having the three of them living there than it had been when they'd had to work ad hoc around unpredictable work schedules. Jilly had finally had enough when Adam had suggested she 'go away to that nice nursing home for a bit and have a rest, like the GP had suggested.' *His* GP, that is, not hers, had also suggested she needed to see a psychiatrist and Jilly wondered how he could possibly know, given that she'd never met him. 'Another of Adam's lies, I suppose,' she decided. She phoned her mother as soon as he'd gone out, packed their bags and they'd relocated.

2015

They were happy enough staying with her mother. After all, Laura had had marital problems of her own once and as for the kids, well, they liked the chaos of Granny's house and the peace that came with the absence of their parent's rows. Jilly worried about them, though. She'd had a wonderful dad whom she'd loved to bits and hated knowing that Sam and Marina would never know what that felt like. But, she was sensible enough to realise that it was out of her hands. She could only do what she could do. Adam would have to sort his own way through it.

***

Jilly made her way 'home' as soon as she got the message. Her phone was always left in the locker when she was on-shift and she noted with some alarm that it had come through some five hours previously.

She'd been going back once a week ever since moving in with her mother, partly to keep an eye on things – she wasn't at all sure Adam would be any good at coping alone – and partly because she wanted to make sure the place was kept clean, tidy and in good repair in case they divorced and it had to be sold. She always made them an evening meal but mostly, her time was spent hoovering and discarding the mountains of takeaway boxes that were piled high in the kitchen sink.

'Why don't you eat out?' she'd asked him, but he simply replied that his eating habits weren't – never had been – any of her business. He didn't want to see the children and expressed no interest in her welfare.

'You've made your decision. We'll see how long it is before you come begging to be allowed back.' Ah. That was how he intended to play it. So be it.

2015

The ambulance had left by the time she got there but there was still a minimal police presence.

'I'm Jilly Jacobs,' she told the constable outside her front door. She was allowed in and informed of the morning's events.

It appeared that Annie, from next door, had been worried that she'd not seen any sign of life for a few days, so she'd used the spare key to check he was okay. Not finding anything downstairs but an uneaten meal, she went up to the bedroom and found him very dead. She immediately phoned the police and an ambulance and attempted to contact Jilly, as had the police and paramedics. All efforts to find her had been unsuccessful and here she was, responding to voice messages from both her neighbour and her mother.

Over the next few days, she discovered that he'd been found in a compromising situation – best not to go into detail – that had gone awry. He'd been dead a few days. There was no suggestion of foul play.

She went next door for a coffee once the police left that morning. 'It must have been terrible for you. Thank you for looking out for him. I wasn't due in again for a couple of days and heaven only knows what sort of state he'd have been in by then. It must have been bad enough as it was.'

'It was a shock. But to be honest, neither Bobby nor I ever really liked him and we won't be sorry to see him go,' Jilly raised her eyebrows but said only 'the house was so tidy and clean, nothing like it usually is when I get there to check on him. He must have gone pretty well as soon as I left last time.'

Annie looked her straight in the eye. 'Oh, without a doubt. The dinner you'd cooked him was still on the kitchen table untouched. I cleared it all away and left the kitchen how you'd want it to be seen by a stranger.'

Ah, thought Jilly. The hot, hot curry with the poison in it – odourless, colourless and leaving no trace after ingestion. Untouched. Cleared away before the police and ambulance arrived. No evidence of it. No chance of it ever being found. Lady Luck was on her side.

She and Annie tacitly acknowledged that they understood each other. They both knew exactly what examination of the contents of the plate would have revealed. There was an unspoken understanding that no reference to it would ever be made again.

The little seaside town was charming. Right off the tourist trail because there was nothing there for them. The pub was pleasant enough but it only served Pub Grub and wasn't child-friendly, the village shop was okay for emergencies but stocked to cater for locals, not outsiders and the post office was open only two mornings a week.

They'd had to search a long time, because their needs were so specific – a two up, two down for Laura and a four bedroomed house for Jilly, next to each other and with no chain involved – but it had been worth the wait. Laura had had a stair-lift put in but apart from that, it was perfect. The children, able to go to the beach every day, were in heaven.

Now in their first year at secondary school, they needed less supervision than they had done and in any case, Jilly had found herself a job as a lab assistant in the local sixth form college – a much better option, she felt, for two kids with a widowed single parent than being a paramedic would have been. Jilly was pleased that she could keep a closer eye on her mother, given that she was now over eighty, although frankly, she looked and behaved like a forty year old.

The whole family were going to Barbados for a month in the school holidays to visit Laura's 'almost brother-in-law and his wife'. The children had never met their uncle and aunt; and neither Jilly nor Laura had seen them since Tom's funeral.

The two women were enjoying a stroll along the beach, when Jilly turned to her mother and said 'Do you remember what you used to tell me as a child? That old saying, "everything comes to those who wait?" Well, they got that right, didn't they?'

Laura had to agree that yes, they had. For Jilly, there were no more antidepressants, the blood pressure had regulated itself, it was a couple of years since she'd had a migraine attack and now that she was living a more regular life and could eat better, even the multi-vitamins had been given the Order of the Boot. And as for Laura – well, her current project was learning to gild. Given how the patterns in her life had fallen, it seemed appropriate that her days were occupied learning how to paint pictures in gold.

TIME TO WAKE UP

Well, you won't recognise me, of course. Not now my hands are like emery boards and I've got blotchy skin. That's all the fudge, I expect. Compensatory gluttony, they call it.

One hundred years of blissful sleep and oh! such wonderful dreams! I had two favourites that I dreamed over and over again; and I can remember them vividly, even today. One of them – well, I can't tell you about that, because it's not the sort of thing nice girls talk about. But the other one – I went down to the beach, collected loads and loads of driftwood and Octopus and the snails helped me build the most exquisite, magical boat. They towed me out onto the water – it was lovely, bobbing up and down on the waves; but the best thing was that you could see through the bottom and the sea underneath was as clear as air on a bright spring morning. I used to sit there on the little bench Octopus had constructed and watch the wonderful creatures below, all living together and getting on with life in their quiet, watery world. Things got eaten, of course they did, and that's not fun. Honestly, I know that no-one wants to be eaten but they only ever ate what was needed to survive. They didn't eat each other just because they were there or so that some other creature couldn't. And they all understood that and accepted it. There was the odd squabble over mating rights but that's evolution, I suppose.

TIME TO WAKE UP

Anyway, there I was, happily dreaming my gorgeous dreams and then this Prince came along, slobbering all over me with a big grin on his face, like 'Aren't I clever. I know how to kiss'. Doh... And of course, I had to be as grateful as anything because I'd been dragged away from my beautiful wonderland to take part in this jamboree called Life.

So here I am. Preparing another meal for Prince C to woof down in five minutes before he takes his sword and goes off fencing or something. Have you noticed, females bear the next generation, cook for them and keep everyone alive and then the chaps go off and try to kill them all? What's that all about? Is this how they entertain themselves? Because let me assure you, it's not with their wives they get their entertainment. Oh no, he made that clear as soon as we left the church. 'We have wives to get heirs,' he told me. 'For anything else, we go elsewhere,' he said. So, naturally, I said 'Oh good! Then it's okay for me to go off and get my pleasure elsewhere, too. Happy Days!' I had visions of all the adventures waiting for me in the outside world. 'Oh no you don't!' he told me. 'If you do that, how will we know that the heirs are really ours and not the woodcutter's sons?' So that was that. It's been nothing but cooking and cleaning ever since.

The real tipping point came when he came back with some undergarments hardly worthy of the name. They were the sort you only put on so they can take them off. You know the sort of thing, they wouldn't even keep your fingernails warm in an English castle. So I thought, 'I've had enough of this. I'm going to form a Union.' And I got in touch with Rapunzel, Cinderella and the rest of the gang and we're going to organise ourselves and tell the world what it's really like.

Because you know what, chaps, we can look after ourselves. That's not to say we don't want you. Of course we do. We don't want to be your enemies. We want to be your friends and lovers, mothers and companions. We just don't need you to save or rescue us. The question I'd like to put, though, is can you save yourselves?

I guess I'll have to come back in the twenty first century to get the answer to that one.

JESSICA

A fairy tale for the twenty first century.

Jessica had always believed that if you're nice to people and treat them kindly, they'll return the compliment.

She couldn't understand, therefore, why people had taken to ignoring her. She'd never been popular, that she knew, but things were being taken to a new level. She'd dropped out of the beach litter pick, because no-one would talk to her and she was starting to feel lonely. Whilst she'd always been quite insular, it'd been a choice and she'd enjoyed it. But, this wasn't a good feeling.

'I wonder what I've done,' she thought, as she wandered along the beach. The waves were very gentle and soothing. If she sat on the sand and just watched them, they were mesmerising.

But today, even that didn't help. The sound and smell of the sea was intoxicating and that, at least, she could rely on.

On her afternoon walk, she kept out of everyone's way. She didn't want to be snubbed. It only made her feel even more sad. She took the meadow road, away from the coast for a change. It wasn't the best time of year to do it, because the flowers had all gone over and it'd been cut back ready for winter. But, it was still a nice enough route to take. 'At least people stay away once the summer's over, so there won't be anyone around to make me feel worse than I do already,' she decided. She stopped thinking about how horrible it was not to be liked and concentrated on the feel of moving through the air, the many different shades of green, the autumn sun moving through the sky. Things weren't that bad, not really.

***

Outside the crematorium, large crowds were gathering. There was a lot of chatter, most of it warm and friendly, in spite of the sadness of the occasion. It was clear that the hall would be packed and a lot of people left standing. As she glanced at them all, Jessica couldn't help hoping it would be a short funeral, because if all those mourners had to stand for ages, well, some of them didn't look that young. 'I wonder how it feels to have so many people wishing you well,' she thought. Whoever this person was had been much loved. 'I think I might pop in on the way back, see what the service is like. I've got plenty of time before I need to get home.' Sometimes, they asked her to play the organ but she hadn't been approached this time – another blow to her self-esteem. 'I mean, I know I'm a good organist and people don't have to talk to me when I'm playing, do they?'

Jessica was a stickler for punctuality. She'd said she'd be back at five, although the evening's piano lessons weren't due to start until five thirty. There were four that day, all of them an hour long, so she needed to pick herself up ready for a concentrated few hours of teaching. Not all her students were that good and sometimes, it could feel like pushing water uphill, but tonight, there was only one who wasn't really making the grade and she was so enthusiastic, it made up for any shortfall in talent. One of them, Liam, could make it in the profession (if he put his mind to it) but he wanted to be an engineer, so that was that. Still, he'd always have the music to ease his way through life.

'At least whatever I did to upset everyone, it hasn't made the students cancel,' she thought and then quickly put the notion aside. After all, she had no assurance they'd turn up until they stood on her doorstep.

There were a few autumn blossoms in the gardens: cyclamen, mostly, but a few nerines and the remains of the dahlias. Autumn always made her feel a bit sad. She loved the beautiful groves of colour the trees made, the quality of the light was different, but even though she tried to tell herself that things were just getting ready to sleep for the winter and renew themselves for the spring, it felt to her as if everything was dying. Winter wasn't so bad, because she doubled the bird food and had any number of visitors, all taking advantage of the unexpected bounty to be found scattered across the lawn and making the feeders almost burst. There was a lot to be said for keeping in touch with nature and the rhythm of the seasons. It kept you in touch with life itself.

***

She'd forgotten about the funeral, so she was brought back to earth with a jolt when she walked past the crematorium again and there were people hanging around outside who she recognised from earlier. They made their way in just as she was approaching the doors and as she peeked through, she saw it was absolutely packed. Every seat was taken and even the spare standing space was sparse. 'Whoever this is for must have led a wonderful life. Some people just have the knack, don't they. It's like they can't help but be loved.' She hung around at the back, not wanting to push her way in, and did her best to look like a piece of wallpaper.

'..... was a wonderful and well-loved person. Always ready to help, to lend an ear and to give refuge to anyone who needed it. In all the years I knew her, she never judged, either me or anyone else. I feel truly privileged to have known her.' Jessica recognised the speaker as her friend, Joel. So, there was a good chance she'd known the deceased, as well. She looked round the congregation. Wow, there was Brenda, and over there was Trixie with her new squeeze, Kieran. Jessica hoped they were happy together. Scanning the crowd again, she saw loads of people she recognised and wondered why no-one had let her know that this funeral was taking place. It must be someone she, too, had been acquainted with. 'Oh well, I guess that'll be something else I'll have done wrong. Not pitching up to a funeral of a dear friend.' She brought her attention back to the next eulogy – how many people were going to get up and sing this woman's praises? There seemed to be no shortage of buddies and well-wishers eager to say their piece.

'..... helped me through some of the darkest times. She was also a great teacher, mentor and guide. I wouldn't be where I am now without her.'

***

Two weeks earlier

'It's a good thing that chocolate has no calories on a Sunday.' Jessica was staring at her cappuccino. The layer on the top was almost worth what she'd paid for it even if you ignored the coffee underneath. 'And broken biscuits of course. And anything at all that someone else

A FAIRY TALE FOR THE TWENTY FIRST CENTURY.

pays for.' This line of thought kept her brain occupied for some time.

She stared out to sea. It was flat calm, unusual at this time of year. There was nothing on the horizon. This was more or less expected. There was a lot of Atlantic to negotiate before stumbling on any land to speak of and the passage times of big ships – even small boats – were pretty easy to predict.

She went and sat next to a rock pool, marvelling at all the creatures in it. She thought of all her mistakes, all the faux pas and the times she'd wished she could have done better.

She wondered how it felt to be loved and valued. 'If I were to get up now and make my way into the water, I could walk right out to sea and nobody would miss me at all,' she concluded. Now, that's something to think about.'

***

The police said it was a tragic accident. The body had washed up a few hours later, to be found by a holiday maker walking his dog.

JESSICA

'She must have fallen asleep on the sand. When the tide came in, she breathed in some water and drowned even before she was swept out on the current.'

Everyone had accepted that it was, indeed, deeply unfortunate that she'd been taken unawares like that both for her and the community she was part of.

'So much to offer and so many people left behind with a big gap in their lives,' said Brenda to Joel when they left the crematorium.

'Oh, Jessica! How will we all manage without you?' she heard Joel exclaim.

Jessica? They knew another Jessica? She'd never known that. Then, she noticed the Order of Service clutched in Brenda's hand, displaying a very clear photograph of herself on its cover.

'Oh god!' she gasped, throwing her hands up to her head in a gesture of despair. 'That's why they've all been ignoring me! I'm dead! They can't see me! So much grief, so much unhappiness and all because of me!'

***

'What do I do now?' she wanted to know. 'I can't stay here. But I've not gone over to wherever I need to be.' She sat down beside a rock pool and stared out at the sea. After a few minutes, she got up and walked into the water.

It was starting over again.

Jessica realised that although she was dead, she hadn't passed on. 'I'm still here and that can't be right. Surely I should be somewhere light and floaty, with angels sitting on clouds

A FAIRY TALE FOR THE TWENTY FIRST CENTURY.

playing trumpets and harps. At least somewhere different from here.' She must have unfinished business and, she thought, until I've done what I'm supposed to do, I'll be trapped. 'How do I find out if no-one can talk to me?' she pondered.

She'd been concerned by all the sadness she'd witnessed at her funeral. 'It's not right. All those people there saying all those things about me. None of them were true. They were being kind.' But then, she thought, that's what people have to do. Mustn't speak ill of the dead. Everyone knew that.

One thing she liked about being dead, now she was getting used to it, was that all she had to do was think about somewhere or somebody and she'd be there with them, able to listen in. The first time this had happened was when she was thinking about Jodie. She found herself sitting next to her on the sofa with Jodie and her sister. 'This is interesting,' she said, confident that neither woman would hear her. 'I didn't know she had a sister or that her name was Karen, but I know now, even though we've never been introduced.'

'If only Jessica were here,' Jodie was saying. 'She'd know what to do.'

'I never knew her but so wish I had. No-one ever has a bad word to say about her,' was Karen's reply.

'And no-one ever did when she was still here. I never knew anyone who was loved like Jess was. Only she hated us calling her that, so I mustn't do it just because she's dead.'

'I don't care,' screeched Jessica, to no avail whatsoever. 'Call me anything you like!'

It didn't help. She couldn't make herself heard and it was too frustrating to be there, listening to this tale of woe. She left them to it.

She went back to the beach, as this was the place where everything had been triggered. Would she discover here what she had to do to complete her mission? But it seemed not. All the discussions with the gulls, oyster-catchers and terns didn't yield anything of any use and although all the dogs tried to talk to her and were doing their best to offer advice (that much was obvious) she couldn't understand a word. 'All the animals understand each other but apart from the birds, it's unintelligible to me. Will I learn to understand them in time? I'd love that. To be honest, as much as I love the birds, their conversation is a tad on the dull side.' She hoped they hadn't heard her thinking but they were still friendly and appeared to bear no grudge, so she decided they probably hadn't.

Now she was used to being dead, it wasn't quite so bad. She still had to walk into the sea on a regular basis, feeling the waves wash over her, drawing her further and further out, the current sucking her down, the water entering her lungs and the slow loss of consciousness. It really wasn't at all pleasant, but like many things, once you got used to it, it was tolerable and stopped being frightening. She'd been surprised in that she'd been totally sure she didn't want to be here anymore, didn't want to endure any further heartache and self-doubt nor be trapped in the isolation she'd chosen for herself, but when the time came, all she wanted was for it to stop and to carry on her life at the point before she started that last, short journey. Maybe that's why she was still here, even though she was dead. Perhaps there was no unfinished business after all just a life completed before its time.

***

After several months of travelling the globe and seeing sights and hearing sounds she'd never even dreamed of, she realised that this was much worse than anything she'd had before the walk into the waves. That feeling of leaden loneliness. After all, everyone she'd known was still alive and if that wasn't enough, they were all saying how much they missed her and found it difficult to imagine they'd never see her again. That made it all so much more intense. 'I walked into the sea because nobody like me and I caused nothing but trouble. Now they all feel guilty and they're saying how much they loved me. I don't like this. I want to go on to wherever I should be.'

She sat on the beach, waiting for the waves to come up high enough for her to start her walk, but it wasn't the right time, so it didn't happen. She waited and waited. The dogs wanted to play with her but she didn't know how. After all, they were flesh and blood and although she'd tried, she couldn't even stroke them.

In a moment of madness, she decided to go back to the clinic and eavesdrop on the conversation in the staff room.

'It'll be a year next week since Jessica Truman died. Sad. She was a nice woman,' said Watson, who'd been her counsellor for a while.

'Sad indeed. A lovely woman but with such a harsh super-ego. Do you think it really was a tragic accident or deliberate?'

'Who knows? I don't want to believe she intended to die. She'd been doing so well. She was bright and cheerful a lot of the time in spite of thinking everyone hated her. And there were the odd little insights into the fact that the people around her really cared, really appreciated her.'

'What a travesty it is, mental illness. What a mess it creates.' Doc Rani knew what she was saying was totally inadequate, but what else could be said?

Jessica realised with the most horrible bump that she'd been wrong all along. When people told her they enjoyed her company, they did. When she was invited out, it wasn't out of pity but because they wanted to share some time with her. So many things flooded through her in that

JESSICA

moment and she was suddenly aware of the suffering her passing had caused but more than that, she was aware of her own worth and importance in the world.

A tiny baby just about to enter the world in Hawaii suddenly received the gift of a soul. When her doting parents held her for the first time, 'Jessica,' said her mother, 'I want to call her Jessica.'

'Perfect,' said Dad. 'She looks exactly like a Jessica.'

And so it was that there were no more treks into the sea, no more self-doubting, no more continual anguish about all the stupid and unforgivable things that had been carried out by the once dead Jessica.

When her time came again, it was peaceful and content, at the end of a full life well lived.

The moral of the story? After all, every fairy story has to have a moral – I think I'll leave you to make your own mind up.

DR BROCK

The knock at the door was nothing special. I mean, people come by unsolicited every day – friends, the postman, the guy wanting to know if I'd like to change my energy supplier. It was no big deal.

I put my coffee down, made my way along the passage and braced myself for whomsoever it might be.

'Long time, no see,' he offered, walking past me straight into the kitchen. 'What have you been up to that's kept you away from the Riverbank?'

I'd better explain. It was Water Rat who was standing there by the dining table, smiling broadly and greeting me like a long lost pal.

Now let me make something clear. I am NOT a mole. Nor a badger nor a toad. I don't live underground spending disproportionate lengths of time doing spring cleaning and have never in my life struck up an acquaintance with Ratty. Or maybe Voley would be better, as we know now that Mr Graham was writing about a water vole and not a rat at all. Come to that, I live in the middle of a big city and to my knowledge, the only riverbank has reinforced concrete along the sides and big notices saying 'Trespassers Will Be Prosecuted. THIS INCLUDES YOU' – with a big hand and a finger pointing straight at you. Most rude, but it does the trick because no-one ever goes there anymore.

'You're very quiet,' he said. 'Weren't you expecting me?'

DR BROCK

'Well frankly, no,' I stuttered back. 'It's just that we don't get too many English-speaking Water Rats here. Not at all, really.' And then I remembered my manners. 'Cup of tea?' I enquired.

'Nothing could make me a happier Rat,' he replied, taking his pipe out of his pocket and lighting up. No question of 'could I?' or 'do you mind if I....?' Just bold as brass started smoking his pipe. 'And a piece of that excellent fruit cake you always have in the tin, if you please!'

How did he know I make fruit cake? But he was right. Every Saturday afternoon, I lay out all the ingredients on the worktop and make my cake for the week. Very good it is, too.

I cut him a slice and gave him a pot of tea to himself. I don't drink it much. The occasional cup, yes, but it's not my favourite. The cake was gone so fast I wouldn't have believed he could swallow quickly enough but there we are. He held the plate out to me and nodded toward the tin, again smiling so affably I couldn't even think of saying no.

These visits became something of a regular interlude in my otherwise not-that-fascinating week. Things are okay. I want for nothing and by and large have a pretty good time. We all know life gets a bit jaded, so it's just ordinary really, what we expect once the flush of youth is past and we have to be responsible adults.

He was good company. There were so many tales of the riverbank and he had any number of adventures with Toad, Badger and Mole. I wished sometimes I could join them but how could I? I don't belong in the Wild Wood or the River. I'm not a boat person or a forester and most definitely don't move in the grand circles that Toad does. I don't even belong in the W.I, even though I do my best to fit in with them. They're nice people but just not right for me.

DR BROCK

My friends all thought I was a bit odd even before Ratty started turning up, so you can see what sort of person I am and these tete-a-tetes were doing nothing to improve my image.

***

Daisy came with me in the end, to make sure he got an accurate picture, so she said, but I thought it was probably because she didn't think I'd go if I were left to my own devices.

'She's been like this ever since she last came to see you. Told us all that there's a new doctor at the Practice called Dr. Brock and that you reminded her of a badger.' That embarrassed me. I mean, fancy telling the poor man that! Still, he didn't seem to mind. He's probably had worse things said to him. Daisy, for her part, couldn't see the resemblance. 'She keeps calling me Toady – *once, I called her Toady. Once, and she never lets me forget it* – and claims that she's being visited by the Water Rat. Is there anything you can do?'

'Well,' said Dr Brock, 'there are a few simple question and answer tests, but first, can you tell me if she's doing silly things that could put her in danger? Or put anyone else in danger?' You could see that Daisy was falling under his spell. He's very unusual to look at. Not tall, dark and handsome but mesmerising and sturdy looking, like he'd be able to look after himself and you as well, if the necessity arose. And he had one of those white forelocks. 'Nominative determinism' was what Daisy called it. He was called Brock so he had a badger streak in his hair. Not quite the same, when I looked it up, but it was clear how she'd made the mistake.

DR BROCK

Anyway, he asked me all these questions that had absolutely no relevance to anything, marking off the answers on a score sheet. Then he wanted to know if I took any over-the-counter remedies for anything, all that sort of stuff. Then he asked: 'And the Water Rat. What's the story with him? Is he affecting your ability to live life the way you usually do?'

'Well,' I said, 'he's okay. Friendly and delightful in his own way. And no. Of course he doesn't affect my life, only in that it's nice to have him to chat to. Now that I'm used to him, naturally. It was a bit of a shock at first and I was worried in case I was going round the bend. But now, well, I think I might miss him if he didn't keep coming back.'

'See Doctor?' interjected Daisy. 'She's like this all the time. Says she can't go out on a Saturday afternoon in case she misses his visit.'

DR BROCK

'But it's doing no harm,' said Dr Brock. 'Why don't we just leave things for a bit and see if they sort themselves out on their own?'

'That seems –' I tried to say something myself but Daisy butted in again.

'I'm worried, Doctor. What shall I do if things get worse?

'If that happens, you know where I am. Phone and make an appointment and I'll be sure to fit you in.'

Daisy agreed to the plan, all the time making it clear she wasn't at all keen on this Dr Brock and his funny way of dealing with things.

We left the surgery and made our way home.

***

Once the two women had left, Dr Brock took his work costume off, opened the trap door in the consulting room floor and scuttled off back to his sett.

Inspired by The Wind in the Willows by Kenneth Graham

THE PODCAST

'.....that men will never be as emotionally intelligent as women.'

Amelia was listening to the radio on the way home. She'd channel hopped and liked this guy's voice. It sort of entered through your ears and made its way down to your toes, causing them to tingle. It had been an interesting podcast and an antidote to the afternoon.

She'd spent it with Tamsin. Her precious Saturday, almost over and all she'd achieved was a supermarket shop. The last few hours didn't count, having been passed listening – well, half-listening, if she was honest – to yet another tale of woe and broken hearts. How many times could one woman fall in love in the course of a year? And for goodness' sake, it was only May.

'But I loved him, Mel, and he promised he'd phone.'

'Mm,' had been the only reply she could muster, and somehow she felt that that probably wouldn't be enough to satisfy Tamsin's needs.

'I mean, I really believed he was The One.'

'The One?' thought Amelia. 'How many "Ones" can there be? I didn't even realise that in this part of the twenty first century, 'The One' was a concept anymore. But maybe, given this must be the tenth or eleventh One this year – that makes an average of two a month – ' she noted, 'the idea of The One has survived after all.'

THE PODCAST

Tamsin had joined a dating site and was working her way through every man who was the right sort of age. It was absolutely true that these blokes were pretty desirable but maybe she could consider delaying the consummation of desire a bit? Take a bit of time to get to know them slightly better? Thought Amelia. It felt to her that they weren't necessarily looking for the right woman to share their lives and bring up children with after all, even though it was what they claimed. Still, who was she to judge? She'd been with the same chap for years, so she had no real yardstick to measure against.

Poor Tamsin, she thought. Finding a mate at their age wasn't going to be that easy. Most people were paired off in some way and the available ones were only really available because they weren't that interested in finding The One at all but looking for a bit of commitment-free distraction from the reality of everyday living.

She popped into the chip shop and bought her evening meal. Who cared about the calories? Indulging in a bit of comfort food once in a while was exactly the thing to do. Dan was visiting his parents for a couple of weeks and she'd got to the stage where she missed him. The first few days were always wonderful but then the pangs started to creep through and she wished he were here to bounce ideas off and snuggle up to when the need arose.

She'd bought herself a magazine in the supermarket and was going to have a quiet weekend, slobbing around and doing nothing. The cleaning could wait.

***

The sound of the key in the lock brought her back to the here and now. She was totally lost in Classic FM's evening offering and although she knew Edie would be getting home from work at some point, she thought it would be a bit later and was enjoying the soft, soothing sounds before the inevitable disturbance of the peace. Edie was a lovely person and without a lodger, there'd be no hope of paying the mortgage. She'd struggled hard to get the deposit together and it stuck in the craw that things had changed so drastically that without a second source of income, she wouldn't be able to keep up the monthly payments.

This evening was going to be a double whammy. Edie had spent the weekend with her family and gone straight to work on her return. Better brace herself.

'The little shit was laughing at me all weekend. He wouldn't leave me alone. I mean, it's only a haircut. Why wouldn't he let the subject drop?' pleaded Edie.

'I don't know. Maybe he liked the response he was getting from you?'

'And if that wasn't enough, mum and dad were on his side. They're always on his side. "He's only a child, Edith. Cut him some slack." Why should I? If he doesn't learn now, when will he?'

'I'm not sure, Edie. Have you tried talking to your parents about him, I mean properly talk, not just rant?'

'I don't rant, Amelia. How can you suggest it?'

'Sorry. My mistake. There's enough supper here for both of us, would you like to share?' She would have preferred a pleasant evening on her own with a meal that wasn't going to end up in indigestion, but it wasn't going to be that way, so maybe just get on with it and hope her frustration wouldn't result in gastric reflux.

'... and then she came back at me and told me that the report just wasn't up to scratch. I've got to do it all over again. A four hundred page report!' Amelia realised she'd drifted off somewhere, because this revelation brought her back with a thud.

'Can't you just edit what you've done already?' She was doing her best but this evening meal had gone on far too long and she simply couldn't find a way of leaving the table to chill out. She wasn't crazy about her own job but had to do it because otherwise, it'd be back to renting a bedsitter. It was well paid work and was getting her the things she wanted. Another twenty two years though. Hopefully things would get better.

'Or maybe you could start looking for another job' she suggested.

Edie looked horrified. 'But I *love* my work, Amelia, how could you suggest it?'

'Well, you seem to hit an awful lot of difficulties. There must be somewhere more pleasant for you to work.'

Amelia yawned.

'I'm sorry if I'm boring you,' replied Edie, very clearly thinking the apology should be coming to her, not from her. She shoved the chair away and stormed up the stairs, slamming the door into her bedroom.

Oh well, thought Amelia. My turn to do the washing up again. Glancing at the clock when everything was again in order, she flopped down on the sofa. 'Another evening gone. Why can't they see the patterns they're creating? Maybe it's easier as an outsider than if you're stuck in the centre of it all.'

She switched on the TV. Another repeat from an age old detective series but at least it required no thought. She knew who did it as soon as the cast list came up on screen.

***

THE PODCAST

Amelia had been pouring her heart out to Dan for over an hour. She kept trying to stem the flow but it just wouldn't stop coming. There'd been more phone calls and more fuming from her friends and she needed to get it all off her own chest.

'You know what,' said Dan, 'it seems to me that maybe you should try to do things a bit different.' He knew he was on thin ice here, but he'd watched this happening for years now and wanted to help her find ways of making things less stressful for herself. 'Maybe find ways of limiting things. Do what mum's friends do. They get together and each of them has five minutes to moan about their aches and pains, then they're not allowed to mention them again. They do things they like doing, like going for a meal or visiting a garden centre.'

Visiting a garden centre? Thought Amelia. I'm not that old yet. She was not best pleased.

Dan realised he hadn't come up with the best example. 'Well, not a garden centre, not at our age (secretly, he liked garden centres with their cheerful colours and optimistic slant on the future) but you know what I'm saying. Something that you and your friends like doing, whatever that is. Go to a show maybe, or learn Italian. Anything that you enjoy doing together. And if that doesn't work, maybe make yourself a little less available?'

'Are you suggesting I ghost them?' Amelia couldn't believe her ears. How like a man to come up with that as a solution.

'Not ghost them, no. Just don't be available all the time. Put the brakes on. Say no sometimes.'

In the tube on Monday morning, she thought about what Dan had said. It'd ruined the weekend and it was such a special one, the first since he'd returned from his parents. She didn't like being criticised like that but, she thought, possibly he had a point. The patterns were there for her to see but she'd missed them too.

She thought back to the podcast. She'd never argue with the guy being interviewed. He knew what he was talking about. He wasn't just a lovely voice, at all. Far from it. He'd spoken masses of good sense and made it all so clear and obvious. But she wondered how he'd come to his conclusions. 'He must have known different women from me, I guess, or possibly he's using different criteria to base his opinion on.'

She got off the train and made her way to the office. As she walked in, her heart sank. It was time to take her own advice and start looking around for another job.

THE SOOTHSAYER'S TALE

It got out of hand, really. It was only supposed to be for a few weeks, while I got the money together for a pair of Louboutin shoes. They were six hundred quid even in the sale and although I had a good job – head nurse in a mental health day centre – I couldn't splash that sort of cash on 'just' a pair of shoes on my salary.

They were officially called sneakers, but they were really, really lovely and I simply adored the idea of having a pair of good shoes for swanning around in at work all day. I know they'd probably just look like a pair of market stall trainers to anyone else seeing them but I knew they'd make me feel good.

Anyway, I went in and he asked me if I had any experience, so I said 'of course'. I'd read tarot cards at various fairs and fundraising things for charity. I'm a volunteer at the donkey sanctuary and they always need extra ways of raising a bit of cash. So anyway, he asked me to read his cards and I got lucky. I told him what sort of house he lived in – not that difficult to make up really, and what sort of car he drove (it was a pretty safe bet that it was his parked outside where he'd be able to keep an eye on it all day) and described his wife. 'Spot on,' he said. 'When can you start?'

So that's how I became Debbie Divine. It was only on Saturdays, when tourists and locals alike pitch up. I got some quirky clothes from the charity shop, changed my make-up and tied my hair up in a silk scarf I found at the back of the cupboard. I had a feeling it'd come in handy one day though I'd envisaged its future being in the shape of a duster. My sister bought it for me one Christmas, and it irritated me at the time, because she knows I don't wear 'posh'. Anyway, it was just the thing and I arrived at 9.45, like he asked me to, and got my schedule. It was pretty full-on. I had clients every hour on the hour all day, and when I asked him about lunch, he said I'd only have them in for forty five minutes each, so I could get a bite to eat and something to drink in the fifteen minutes between. It worked out okay, as it happens. You run out of things to say sometimes.

He charged the clients fifty quid a reading and I got thirty five of that. That was two hundred and eighty a day. If I did it for a month, I'd be able to buy two pairs of Louboutins, so I was on to a good thing. I didn't tell anyone at work. They'd never approve. We'd talked about it in the past over tea breaks and lunches and they all agreed it was conning vulnerable people out of their money, but honestly, I didn't see it like that. If anyone came in genuinely distressed, I'd tell them I could see nothing and give them their money back, even though it meant I'd lose out on the deal, but there weren't many of them. Most of them just saw it as a bit of fun and didn't take it all that seriously.

It got so popular, he asked me if I'd go in on Sundays but I had to have a day off, so I said no. Apparently, people were coming in and asking if they could see Debbie, because they'd heard she was the best. He wasn't happy, because it was a good earner for him. I mean, the room would have been empty all day otherwise and he had to do nothing for the hundred and twenty pounds he got in commission. I even had to do my own cleaning, except that apart from a few crumbs from the sandwiches I took in, it didn't really get dirty, so it wasn't such a big deal. Anyway, he decided that if I was that good, he'd put the price up to sixty and I could have forty. I told him I didn't think it was a good idea, it'd put people off but he said that they'd been saying they'd spend a hundred if he could entice me in to do more hours. That took me by surprise. I mean, have you ever seen tarot cards? It's quite true that there are LOADS of different sorts but if you choose a pack with pictures on, you can make up a story to go with them and it doesn't even take that much imagination. But there we are. Maybe I've got a gift after all.... No, I don't think so, either.

Anyway, I was enjoying myself. All those people – they were very different from my colleagues at work and the clients, who mostly *are* in genuine distress and you couldn't possibly fob them off with a bit of colourful imagination – were really nice to be with. Even if they weren't, forty five minutes goes ever so quickly. So instead of leaving once I'd got the money together for the shoes, I stayed and started putting it on an account that earned interest so that I could upgrade my car. You need something reliable in my job. It's not good if you turn up late because the car won't start and sometimes, you have to go to a client's house with a CPN or doctor and you don't necessarily start off from the same base.

One Saturday, this woman came in, very frail looking. She was quite tall but so, so thin and I asked her if she was eating enough, and she said she never stopped but she couldn't stop the weight loss. So instead of telling her fortune, I chatted to her about her health and her lifestyle, things like that, and at the end I gave her her money back and told her I thought she should go and see her doctor. I hoped Nigel – the owner – wouldn't hear about it. He'd have a go at me for not giving the customers what they came in for but honestly, what would you have done? The poor woman was obviously unwell and didn't like talking to her friends about the weight loss because 'they had problems of their own.' That always makes me a bit sad. I mean, what are friends for? Only it seemed that it didn't really matter, because a couple of weeks later, another woman came in, only this time she was having problems with her husband and said she wanted to know if she should leave him. Well, I could hardly give her an honest answer, could I? Everyone has problems with their spouses from time to time, so we just chatted about her marital problems and

THE SOOTHSAYER'S TALE

I gave her the names and contact numbers of a couple of helplines I keep on my phone. I gave her the money back, too. I mean, I know I was losing income here, but I couldn't take money from people who needed something more than a bit of fun on a Saturday afternoon. It wouldn't be right.

Things carried on much the same for a good while. I got that new car I'd been saving for and it's great knowing every time I go out of the front door, it'll start first time. Have you ever had that feeling? It's been worth all the lost weekends.

Then, late one Saturday, this bloke came in. Now, that's unusual. You don't see many men coming in for this sort of thing, so I was a bit surprised. He was quite distinguished looking with really intense eyes and thick black hair and he was really unsettling. I even wondered if he'd been sent up from some sort of netherworld to see if he could buy my soul but quickly stamped on that thought. When he sat down, I could see – truly, I could honestly see – knives surrounding him. I was genuinely spooked and just wanted to get rid of him, but I couldn't tell him to naff off, so I got the cards out and tried to do a 'reading'. It was hopeless, so I asked him if there was anything he wanted to talk about, anything he wanted to ask me, and he said yes, he wanted to know what made me think I was a tarot reader. So I said I'd been doing it for a long time and people seemed to like me. He told me he thought I was a fraud. His sister had been in and all I'd done was give her the numbers of a few domestic abuse helplines and that was fine, because she'd phoned one of them and they'd helped her sort herself out and she hadn't taken any notice of him, so I'd helped them all out; but if I was offering counselling, I should get myself some qualifications and set myself up as a counsellor, not a tarot reader. So I told him if he didn't like it he should go and ask Nigel for his sixty quid back, and he said 'Sixty? I just paid a hundred,' and that shocked me, because I hadn't been given a pay rise. I suppose if I was really a soothsayer, I'd have known I was being cheated by my boss. Anyway, on his way out, I called out to him 'your life is going to be changed by a bit of paper' and he just said 'huh' and flounced out.

When I left that evening, he was coming towards the shop and he stopped me and asked if I'd like a coffee with him. He said he'd found a fifty pound note by his car door and thought as it was money he would never have had, he'd see if he could treat me to say thank you for sorting his sister out.

Turns out he's a heart surgeon in London and lives in Hampstead Garden Suburb. He'd brought Marie down here for a few days to get her away from it all and that's how she'd ended up visiting Debbie Divine. I'm moving in with him next month, once I've served my notice and there's loads of work up there, so it shouldn't be that hard getting a job.

I never did buy the Louboutins.

THE LIME TREE AND THE GARDENER

'Will you still love me when the years have turned my hair grey?' she asked.

'Of course,' he replied. 'Change is the child of time.'

'But when I'm old and feeble. Will you still want me?' She felt she was pushing him too hard, making herself appear needy. Who knows? Maybe she was.

'We're nothing without change,' he said. 'Trust me. I'll be there.'

She watched him pack his rucksack and check he had everything he'd need on his travels.

'Trust me,' he said again. 'You won't end your life lonely.'

The days passed, morphing into months and years. Every knock on the door was greeted with an excited whoop of joy. 'It's him. He's back', she thought, but it always turned out to be the postman or the man from the Pru.

With the passage of time, Linden knew she must accept he wasn't coming back. She moved on. Found a father for her children, watched the years pass, made quicker by the growing of her daughters into young women and then mothers themselves.

The knock on the door took her by surprise. Could it be him? She wondered, secretly hoping. But no, of course not. How would he know where to find her now, after all these lifetimes and why would he bother to try? But in spite of that, when she saw the delivery man on the doorstep, her heart plummeted again.

Time made her a widow, a great grandmother; but deep in her soul, she still hoped that somehow, someday, the gardener would return. She looked in the mirror. 'Look at me.' she thought. 'What happened to transform me into this shadow of a woman? Did he take all my dreams with him?' She had no real complaints. Her passage through life had been a happy one, her family healthy and successful. But always, always in the recesses no-one ever penetrated, there was a space for him, waiting to be filled.

Another long, lonely day. Another knock. Another leap of the heart, which – she was sure – would lead only to another sinking once she saw her visitor.

She stared, open-mouthed. For a split second, she was that young, fun-loving twenty-three year old who wished him bon voyage

'But I'm an old woman now. What can you want with me now that I'm used up with nothing left to give?'

'I love – always loved – the tree, not only the blossom,' he replied.

'Too late,' she told him and closed the door.

'Much, much too late,' she said to herself heading to her comfortable armchair by the fireside.

She poured her first – and last – glass of wine, the only one she would ever drink, from the bottle she'd bought and saved to celebrate his return.

'Here's to us,' she said, raising her glass.

She sipped it slowly, settled back into the chair and let the rest of life take care of itself.

Inspired by Die abgebluehte Linde *by Franz Schubert*

BANGER AND THE POODLE

Have you ever come across someone on a regular basis, found them intriguing but never had the opportunity to find out about them, who they are, what makes them tick?

Well, that's what happened to me during that first lockdown. Do you remember it? We weren't allowed to do much at all, just go for an hour long walk, buy groceries, talk to people on the phone and not much else.

I must admit, I cheated a bit and went for two half hour sessions of 'permitted exercise'. As well as an early morning stroll, I walked my neighbours' dog for them. Gorgeous creature. They were both considered to be vulnerable. It wasn't that surprising. They're both pretty ancient and don't find it easy getting around whatever the circumstances. Anyway, this little dog, Banger, he's called – please don't ask me why – he and I used to go for a walk every day. I tried never to take him the same way two days running, only sometimes I had to.

Banger had lots of friends in the area, probably more than I have. Have you ever heard it said that if you walk a dog, you make friends? Well, it never happened to me. I tried to be nice and Banger was certainly popular but there just didn't seem to be much to say beyond good morning and enjoy your walk. I don't suppose being two metres apart helped, when I think of it now. It felt as if everyone loved Banger though. He got so many treats on those walks that I suspected he'd be unable to eat his evening meal but dogs don't seem to be affected by things like that, like they've got stomachs that extend down into their toes.

Anyway, everyone wanted to say hello and give him a little pat or a stroke. Except this one man. He had a shaggy toy poodle and walked around with his head down and his eyes firmly planted on the ground in front of him. I tried saying hello, even asked him if he was okay and getting on alright with the restrictions but he never answered. He wasn't that old, about sixty I suppose although it was difficult to tell. He was never unpleasant or nasty, just didn't want to talk. You have to respect people's choices in life, don't you, so I started to ignore him in the end.

I continued to walk Banger even after the lockdowns had ended and life started to get back to some sort of normality. The neighbours hadn't got any younger during that time and the little lad still needed his daily exercise. We still said hello to everyone we passed and I'd started to buy treats myself to hand out to the other dogs. It seemed a bit mean really, letting Banger have the odd biscuit or meaty morsel and never giving anything back in return.

I hadn't seen the man for ages, but when I saw a young woman walking a poodle, I thought maybe it was the same dog and she was doing what I was and walking him as a favour. So I asked her only she said no, it was her dog and she hadn't seen anyone else with a poodle. Come to think of it, hers was a bit bigger than a toy, only it didn't register at the time.

I had all sorts of theories as to what might have happened to him. Had he moved? Had something happened to the dog? Was he ill himself? I kept asking but no-one knew anything about him at all. In fact, apart from me, there didn't appear to be anyone who'd seen him.

This was getting spooky. I knew he was real. At least, I don't believe in ghosts, so he had to be real. And someone must know who he was and if he was okay. How to find out? I could hardly go to the police and say there was a bloke with a dog I don't see anymore and he might have gone missing or been accosted or something. That really wouldn't go down well at all.

I forgot it for a bit, now that life was definitely more like it used to be – no more working from home, no more days when I could organise my own schedule and take my walk when it felt right for me. It was all commuting and nine to five and grabbing a sandwich at the desk and eating much too late at night, taking Banger for a quick walk so he could do what dogs have to do before he settled down for the night. And if that wasn't enough, we line managers had been asked to submit ideas for a party to thank the employees for all they'd done during the worst of the pandemic. Thank goodness for Banger. He helped to keep me sane.

One Saturday, the two of us were enjoying our walk on the Common, when one of the other dog walkers stopped me. 'If you're still looking for the guy with the poodle, I saw him the other morning. It was quite early, about 5.30. He didn't stop and wasn't interested in any pleasantries. Just kept his head down and kept walking.' 'Thanks,' I replied. 'At least we know they're both still alive.'

I thought of taking Banger out early one day to see if I could catch sight of him, just to check he was okay. Being out at that time, though, it could be that he was trying to avoid other people. For some, it's not a route they want to go down, is it, acknowledging complete strangers in the street. And for some, they'd prefer to live the life of a hermit and never have to bother to interact with others at all. Mind you, when you think of the banal conversations you get into, you can see their point. I mean, one of my most recent chats with my neighbour was the relative merits of different window cleaning products. I got really bored and kept trying to get away, only then it occurred to me that this was the first time I'd seen him in weeks and maybe for him, this encounter was a big deal and meant a lot, so I tried a bit harder. I doubt I was that convincing but you need to give it a go, don't you.

Banger's mum and dad are getting past it, to tell you the truth. I think I'm going to ask them if they'd like me to take the little chap in and bring him to see them every day. Or maybe they could have him during the day and I take over in the evenings until I go to work next morning and ease them and him into having a new home. They love him to bits. I wouldn't want to take him out of their lives. It'd be cruel.

Anyway, this works do came with a three line whip. I hadn't looked forward to it at all, although I'd done my best to get into the right mood. It meant that poor Banger's walk would be even later than usual. I bet the bloke with the poodle never found himself in these situations.

These things get on your nerves, don't they, everyone having to get on with the small talk and eat stale sandwiches and things, but there we are. It has to be done. I just wanted to get back to Banger and the comfort of my own armchair.

Feeling particularly bored, I was surprised to be approached by one of the other line managers.

'Hi there,' he said. 'How's Banger?'

I must have looked confused, because he smiled and said 'I'm the man with the poodle. You don't recognise me out of context, do you?'

No, folks. I hadn't.

***

On the way home, I was in a bit of a quandary. What should I do if I saw him again walking with the poodle, whose name was Basil, by the way, the poodle, not the man. We had quite an interesting conversation about the Common and I really enjoyed it. I think he must have found the party boring too, though, because he didn't seem that comfortable. Turns out he works in Accounts, whereas I'm in Publicity. He's been there years, loads more than me. And of course, I'd need a plan of action in case I saw him again at work. Not that likely, really, Publicity and Accounts don't mix much and the building we work in is massive. I should have asked him, I suppose, but you don't think of everything, do you, especially when you're taken by surprise.

Banger was really pleased to see me that evening. We only went for a short walk, as I was tired, but he didn't seem to mind. He snuggled up to me on the bed and snored like anything. I know we're told that we shouldn't let them do that, but how can you turf them off? I slept well and was refreshed when I got up the next morning.

I decided that the only way I could resolve things was by going up to Accounts and asking him direct.

***

I was never able to track him down. It's such a big department and no-one really seemed to know who I was talking about. I mean, like I said, I hadn't even asked his first name. We'd simply chatted without there seeming to be any need for names. I didn't see him again walking Basil, either, so the problem of how to respond never arose. I did get a letter though, sent to my office address. It was from a solicitor telling me I'd been left something in a will. Seems that George – that was his name – died a couple of weeks after the party. He knew he was on his last legs and as he had no-one, he left something to me. Not a fortune – most of his estate was going to the RSPCA – but enough for me to give up my job and go to university. The solicitor explained that he'd been a lonely man and was moved by the fact that someone had shown interest in him. Most people thought he was a boring, nondescript accountant and didn't consider he was much worth spending time with. Poor George. The solicitor was taking care of Basil and asked if I'd like to go in to meet the two of them.

Basil's a lovely dog and I visit the solicitor and his partner sometimes in his house on the other side of the Common. I always take Banger with me. The two doggies get on like they were born to be together. I'm starting university soon to put right the deficit in my education and I'm hoping it'll lead to an entirely new career.

All of this because of Banger and the poodle. It's absolutely true that walking a dog leads to friendship, however much distance there is between you. The solicitor says he's come across things like this before. Makes you think, doesn't it. All those lonely people just waiting for the chance to connect.

So, don't wait. Smile first, think later. Maybe even get a dog....

GRANNIE LOUIE'S BIG ADVENTURE

Part 4: Time To Say Goodbye

Jake was a multi-millionaire. He wasn't sorry he hadn't opted for a sports science degree. They were two-a-penny these days and competing for work was a nightmare. He'd seen that from his friends. 'One job for every fifty applicants' was what they'd been told at school. He thought it might be a bit of an exaggeration but those classmates who'd gone down that route hadn't ended up working in sport or anything related to it. He'd convinced India she'd be better off following her first love and pursuing a career in veterinary surgery rather than nursing. He was paying her fees as well as providing an allowance. Josie and Rick weren't that happy about it. 'She won't learn the value of money,' they said. They believed that being broke was one of the things you went to university to learn about. 'It's not all about training for a career,' Josie had told them both. 'Life skills are important, too,' Jake didn't take a lot of notice. He owed them nothing nor they him and most of the time, they rubbed along fine.

He was stunned at how the public had lapped up Grannie Louie's stories. Once the book had topped the two million mark, the approach for the rights to create a TV series – and then, a little later, a film – followed really quickly. To say he'd retired early was the art of understatement writ large. He was a young and satisfied man, able to pursue the things in life that gave him fulfilment, just like Grannie Louie had said he should. He gave a lot of his money away, as well as paying for the very best care home there was, now that she'd got a little too unsteady on her feet and was a trifle forgetful sometimes, leaving the gas on or the doors unlocked and open.

'Tell me again how it started, Grannie.' He never tired of hearing these tales of Grannie's make-believe travels.

'Oh Jake. I've told you this so many times.' Secretly, she was delighted to tell them. Jake was the only person who wanted to listen. 'I think I've run out of stories, although I do keep trying to remember new ones.' She judged it best to pretend these events grew out of her imagination rather than insisting they were real. She knew she shouldn't remind him that he'd been there with her for a while. Apart from anything else, if Josie and Rick found out, they'd be asking the staff to have her put on pills and she definitely didn't want that.

Jake sometimes wondered why the name 'Freddie' kept popping into his head and why he could picture the places Grannie talked about so clearly, as if he'd been there himself. 'There must be some reason for it,' he thought. But in the ignorance of their history, he just acknowledged them as they entered his mind and moved on.

***

'Are you going over there again tonight?' asked Abi.

'I thought I might. It'd be nice to see Grannie again before she passes on,' replied Jake. 'If it wasn't for her, we'd have none of all this.' He indicated the house and the car.

'How does he keep his feet on the ground?' wondered Abi. 'Most men of his age with everything he had so young would have gone off the rails.' But what she said was 'Have you told her yet about the baby?'

PART 4: TIME TO SAY GOODBYE

'Not yet love, but I want to tell her, if you're happy for me to.'

'I'd rather wait a bit, just in case, but as you say, she can't last that much longer, so better she knows in case we're too late.'

***

'I really don't know what to tell you,' the doctor informed him. 'She's definitely been gone at least twenty four hours but there are none of the physical signs you'd expect to see in a dead body. In fact, there are bits of her that look as if they're getting younger.' Dr McClean looked at the glowing skin and thick gunmetal hair – 'I could have sworn her hair was white,' she said to herself. I'm not getting enough sleep. Better pop into the chemist on the way home and get some over-the-counter pills'. She couldn't help feeling a slight pang of jealousy. 'I wish my complexion was like that at my age, let alone hers' she thought. She was a good forty years younger than Grannie Louie.

Jake recalled how she'd tell him to concentrate on the moment, live now and then time doesn't matter. Could it be that she was still here with them in some form, just being present only in the 'here and now'. He stopped the thought before he got tangled up in it.

'What shall I do, doctor?' He asked. 'I mean, we'd like to get the funeral arranged. A lot of people want to pay their respects.'

'There are no signs of life, so I'd say "go ahead."' Dr McClean knew that holding up the formalities would help no-one in spite of being absolutely baffled at the situation she found herself in.

As Jake turned to leave the room, he could have sworn he saw Grannie Louie smile.

***

GRANNIE LOUIE'S BIG ADVENTURE

Grannie Louie sat down in her favourite chair. Her work was done. She'd had an absolute ball. 'A life lived in colour, I think I'd call it,' she said, and hoped that's what they'd put on her gravestone. She looked around her. Nothing had changed since she went back down with Jake, except there was no computer console and when she looked at herself, there was nothing to see. 'They told me that up here we could choose to have no material presence,' she said to herself. 'Now that tired old body's worn out, I can forget the flesh for a bit. They can rejuvenate mine and pass it on to Freddie when he's born. For the time being, I'll get on with other things.'

Which is exactly what she did; and when she'd satisfied her curiosity, she filled in the application form and came back down to earth.

I survived the loss of my voice.

I can survive anything

Polly J. Fry

FINALE

THE REBUILD

The realisation that I'd spent far too much time and energy trying to find answers that simply weren't there was quite slow.

***

It's impossible to describe my feelings when I realised I could sing again. Indeed, it's impossible to remember what they were with any degree of accuracy. As we know, emotional memory is even more unreliable than any other type and in this respect, my memory is no better than anyone else's. I do know, however, that the music originating in my 'soul' could again be expressed through my body. At least, that was what I believed at the time. Those few days in the Somerset bungalow were more magical than ever. There was the familiar wrench at having to leave but it wasn't my 'real life' and I couldn't do any singing there, so coming home was as exciting as leaving for my holiday had been.

Unsurprisingly, it didn't pan out the way I'd seen it happening in my head. There was no glorious rediscovery of a singer's life with all the joy - and, at times, pain - that that encompasses; no return to a life focussed on making music with people having the same commitment as my own. In fact, not even a glorious voice.

I'd had sixteen years unable to express myself in music. Now, I was a singer with a voice who was unable to use it effectively. During that time, I'd reinvented myself and was a virtually new me. The process of restoring my singing has been, shall we say, confusing. If you remember, in the introduction the observation was made that voice for a singer is inextricably bound up with self-esteem and self-worth. I'd had to find other ways of establishing both these attributes and had done a reasonable job of it.

Vocally, had I been able to sing through those sixteen years, my voice would have changed anyway, but it would have been imperceptible, as it and I would have evolved together. Now, it was entirely different from the way it had been left behind and I knew I would have to relearn my art.

In the interim, my right kidney had been removed, leaving me with a scar running in an arc from between my breasts, down my torso and curving round to reach its destiny at the top of my right hip. The scar itself is no big deal but the damage to the muscle associated with having been cut through has never been fully repaired, no doubt associated with the fact that building muscle gets more difficult the older we get, so I guess it's more or less to be expected. In respect of singing, it means that support is not quite as it was. Also, as is probably inevitable with the passage of time, my stamina had decreased significantly and singing is an energy-intensive occupation.

In terms of practicalities, there was nowhere to practice, I'd cut myself off from my musical life a long time since and was living on a small island with limited opportunity for making music, had no library of scores and books of songs anymore and apart from starting to play the harp had done nothing with my musical self in many years. Indeed, I no longer even owned a piano. I'm still learning just how badly deskilled I became during the years since the 'accident'. It's clear, then, that the return to a musical life was not going to be straightforward, although it didn't occur to me at the time.

Whilst acknowledging that the instrument was somewhat shoddy, I rather optimistically believed that with work that could be changed. Not that I wanted my 'old' voice back. I knew that would never be a possibility but I wanted to be able to use it as fluently as I had.

I started working on my own, doing the things I would do with a beginning student; but found that not only did I not recognise my voice now but never really knew what was going to come out of my mouth. Some days it would be good enough, others it sounded like someone attempting to sing through a tin can. As well as this, having been a contralto, it came as a surprise to discover that the lower register still resulted in the tell-tale pain across my the right hand side of my neck that had characterised my abortive attempts at singing through the wilderness years, whereas from about the E a third up from middle C, the pain stopped completely; and I could sing higher than I used to. This is not the way round we expect it to be. Most voices go down with age, not up. It was time to look for a teacher.

My first port of call was the teacher I'd done most of my training with. Sadly, she'd died since I last saw her. The only other person I would have gone to at that time lived far too far away for it to be practical. A harpist buddy directed me to someone in Ryde, an extremely good teacher and a lovely woman; but both she and I expected far too much of me at that time and it didn't work.

No-one can understand the anguish of rebirth unless they've been through it, (which, of course, is why I'm writing this). After all, I'd had an excellent training, a career I'd been happy in, probably knew as much about the voice as anyone (almost certainly more than most people), so surely it would be straightforward to put all that into practice. This was one of the many occasions in my life on which I have been proved wrong.

During my search I came across Jurgita, a singer, teacher and conductor who I'd seen in action and liked very much. She helped me in various ways, not least of all in encouraging me to sing a completely new repertoire. She believed I was a soprano and whilst I'm not totally convinced, I enjoy the upper voice greatly. It's a completely different concept of singing (to me) and there isn't the unconscious niggle 'I used to sing this a hundred times better' purely because I never even attempted to sing it before; but I'm rushing ahead. This was much later.

I joined a choir in order to both build my stamina again and revel in music in equal measure but didn't stay because I didn't like the chorus master, which is a shame, as the guy who took over from him was excellent and although I returned briefly, the events of 2020 brought about a closing down of the choir altogether, so there's no hope of going back now things are again relaxed. I tried to find someone who would accompany me just for the pleasure of music making but all those I approached were self-styled experts in vocal matters and all I wanted to do with them was sing, so it never happened.

I spent a lot of time trying to research remedial singing but there is surprisingly little information available. At least, there might be tons out there but I was unable to locate it, and there were certainly no such teachers here on the island. I regretted ditching my books on the singer's throat and chest and to be honest, started to regret moving to the Isle of Wight. I was painfully aware there would be far more available were I living in my old home. Such is life. There had been significant benefits to my relocation and it was important for me to remember that.

There were/are also the problems associated with being deskilled in those things that work in tandem with the voice: performance skills, for a start. I was never a natural performer and it was something that was hard learned, no matter how much I enjoyed it once mastered. Then, there are the 'general musicianship' skills. I could no longer analyse a piece of music just by listening to it; no longer identify a piece and/or its composer from the first note or bars. Indeed, although I recognised a lot of the music I had started to listen to again, I had no clue what it was; and more importantly, could no longer rely on myself to 'feel' with my body where I belonged in a piece and where it was taking me. And my sight-reading, never my best asset, was – and remains - dire. If that isn't enough, my language skills had deteriorated – Italian (apart from pronunciation) had all but gone and French was ragged. Even German was no longer as easy to speak as English, in spite of having spent three years in Hamburg.

However, all was not totally hopeless. A musician friend with whom I had recently re-established contact told me of a colleague of his originally from the island who had now moved back. He was a pianist, accompanist and repetiteur and intended to run his career from down here. I phoned him, we chatted and arranged to meet. This was the start of a somewhat strange but happy collaboration. When I leave his music room, it's with a mixture of joy at making music together and despair that I'm now so bad at it, (although we tend to differ with regard to exactly how bad it is).

***

A friend on the mainland was, at the time, in the throes of a PhD and we chatted about whether it would be a good idea for me to do the same, researching the psychological impact on singers of both voice loss and its reinstatement. It might help me understand what was going on inside me and would certainly be an interesting project. I set to writing a proposal, only to discover that there is no work out there to call upon. My next step was to try to find a supervisor armed with what little I had. It was at this time that I was put in touch with Aparna Ramachandran (mentioned earlier) who was looking for subjects for her own study. She liked the idea of a PhD in the area I wanted to pursue and encouraged me to go forward with the idea.

I contacted various people and organisations, in the end realising that it was never going to happen, so I ditched it – like I said, I've never seen a great deal of point in chasing something that is going to be impossible to catch. Instead, I came up with the idea of writing a book from three different perspectives: mine, that of a psychiatrist with an interest in this general area and a speech therapist. It might (or might not) have been a good idea but I didn't know how to find a psychiatrist interested enough or with sufficient time or both. I did find a speech therapist here on the island and she and I came up with the idea of starting a small voice clinic, with her looking at rehab utilising her vast knowledge and expertise and me looking at vocal technique that would protect the voice in future use. That fell by the wayside, too, for reasons not worth exploring here. I ended up writing this book, which whilst very limited in its scope, does give some small insight into the problems encountered and even if all it does is show someone else with the same experience that they're not alone, it will at least mean that something good has come from it.

***

In spite of how it may appear, I continued to live a full life in addition to trying to find my voice again. I got involved with various projects relating to the environment and the local community and have continued visiting Somerset as frequently as possible. I redesigned the garden and even made a second attempt at learning Hindi, this time considerably less successful than the first had been; also, of course, I have good friends both on the Isle of Wight and mainland Britain, with whom I get together whenever the opportunity arises. So, things are good. I do sing now after a fashion - love singing duets, enjoy my sessions with James and would very much like to be in a quartet, octet or chamber choir. As well as this, I sing at funerals. This last is surprisingly satisfying. My voice will never reach the standard it was but I've ceased to look at it as a battle to get my voice back into shape and more as an exploration to see where I can lead it.

There is much more help out there now than there was back then – the network of Voice Clinics and the British Voice Association to name but two of the organisations. (Contact details are listed at the end of the book.) There are also more teachers specialising in voice rehabilitation. As far as I am aware, though, there is still very limited understanding or help available with the psychological impact of voice loss on singers. It's occurred to me since that it might have been worth talking to a sports psychologist or maybe a psychiatrist with an interest in that field, but it wouldn't have been my first thought and it's not something I'll pursue at this stage. It's an interesting observation, though, that there are any number of psychologists for sport but none for singing. I guess it reflects the relative value our society places on the two pursuits, despite the fact that (as I've been regularly reminded) 'anyone and everyone can sing'.

As I pointed out before, I've always believed that whilst the initial injury was physical, not getting the voice back was psychological, and this is especially true now, as in addition to the obstacles encountered during those sixteen voiceless years, there is not just the recurring thought 'am I going to destroy it again?' but also, 'at this stage of life, what is the point?'

***

So, to sum up: the voice continues to be rough and unwieldy, my musicianship poor through years of neglect, and whether we like it or not, our brains subconsciously compare where we are with where we were. Something that did help, though, was when Jurgita suggested that rather than controlling the voice, I was letting it control me. It caused a shift in perspective that made a big difference.

I considered asking my GP for a referral to either a psychotherapist or a psychiatrist to try to unravel the various strands making the rebuilding process so traumatic, but decided against because I don't judge this to be something worth taking up a psychiatrist's/therapist's time anymore, given that it's no longer causing me any serious distress but it will be clear that singing is still a significant aspect of who I am. Moreover, although I firmly believe that the difficulties with vocalisation I had (and have) are psychogenic, I tend towards the belief that if we want to sort out our problems, the only person who can do it is the individual concerned. (That is, of course, if we're fortunate enough not to experience full-blown mental illness.) Certainly, the only person who can do the work is the individual concerned and in spite of many years working in mental health, I'm not totally convinced that we can ever really know what the 'truth' is, just find rationalisations and explanations that we find acceptable. For me, life is a series of random events and whilst, as *Homo sapiens*, we seek to find patterns and answers, when we do, they're artificial and just as likely to be fantasies as fairies at the bottom of the garden. I will say, though, that had there been a little more support at the time of the initial loss, many of the subsequent (and current) obstructions would not have arisen or at least, would have been less serious. As suggested above, if this were to happen today, there is more help out there both physically and, I don't doubt, psychologically; and the feelings of bewilderment and being alone with a problem that no-one cared about wouldn't be anywhere near as severe, if they arose at all.

Of course, this all sounds as if it's a done deal that the difficulties are purely psychological. I's quite possible that as the instrument itself – along with the rest of me – has undergone many years of wear and tear and that, too, is a major contributor to my vocal problems now. As with most things, separating the physical and mental is never going to be an easy task, if it's even possible.

The bottom line, as I pointed out above, is that I've spent far too long trying to find answers and I'm tired of looking for solutions that probably aren't available. The answer, for me, is to sing, however bad it is, and if I can, to get better at it.

So, that's more or less the end of the story. I am aware that I was extremely lucky and privileged to do as much as I did. I have a satisfying and happy life and the fact that I can use my voice again is a bonus.

As I write, there are blackbirds in the garden squabbling over the mealworms, it's high summer and outside my window is a joyous spectrum of colour and texture. A couple of friends are coming over this afternoon for tea and cake. What is there to complain about?

Your voice is the most potent magic in existence

Michael Bassey Johnson

SWANSONG

Having reread Wyddershyns and spent a lot of time rereading and revising this manuscript, I think it's true to say that those people who asked me to record my life story for posterity have got what they wanted, albeit a very different story from the one they requested.

This is – and was always intended to be – my last excursion into fiction and autobiographical writing. It's been really good fun doing it. There have been some lovely people along the way, interesting, informative and amusing conversations; I've learned a great deal and got much satisfaction from putting these books together. There are still three in the cupboard: one, the second instalment in the lives of Mrs Khan and her friends; the second too raunchy to see the light of day and the third a science fiction story. Unless something mind-blowing and totally unforeseen happens, they'll stay gathering dust for posterity.

I've also had some heart-warming feedback about my writing, the two pieces that touched me most being someone in New Zealand, who said that it was like having a friend in the room confiding in you; and another saying that reading Wyddershyns felt like talking to a trusted friend. I think if I ever wanted to write my own epitaph, it would be something encompassing that general idea. Being a good friend is probably what I would like most to achieve before I shuffle off.

SWANSONG

Those of you who've read Wyddershyns will know that I spend a great deal of time telling the world how lucky I am and how truly blessed to have crossed paths with some amazing people, some of whom have (usually unwittingly) guided me towards a course that would lead to something 'better'. I'm glad to have been able to pay tribute to the eight individuals who had a chapter to themselves in that volume; but there have been many, many others who've been invaluable over the years, and a great many who still are, in spite of not having steered me along another, more suitable track than the one I was following. It would take a book in its own right simply to name them, but I'd like to say thank you to Martin Scotcher and Sera Masera for helping me becoming mobile again, when the odds were against me.

The direction I've chosen for the future is a big departure from what has gone before and will probably take time to get underway. In any case, who's to say there isn't someone out there who'll steer me onto a different, more appropriate path?

I hope you've found bits and pieces in this book that you've enjoyed and maybe you've found the narrative interesting. Either way, thank you for your time and patience. I wish you well in your own endeavours.

Take care.

If I cannot fly, let me sing

Stephen Sondheim

USEFUL CONTACTS

British Association for Performing Arts Medicine
  www.bapam.org.uk
  info@bapam.org
  020 7404 8444

British Voice Association
  www.britishvoiceassociation.org.uk
  administrator@britishvoiceassociation.org.uk
  0300 123 2773
  Among other things, this website gives Information relating to Voice Clinics

The Association of Teachers of Singing
  http://aotos.org.uk
  Email form available online

ACKNOWLEDGEMENTS

Rebecca Brown, for again doing a lovely job with the internal design

Jurgita Leistrumaite, for her faith in me

James Longford, for being infinitely patient and a wonderful musician

Aparna Ramachandran, for the work she is doing on voice loss in singers

Cheryl Russell, for wading through the text and giving me feedback

Ros Whistance, for feedback; and her husband, **Dave**, for his patience.

All the friends and acquaintances who've been there throughout, with kindness and forbearance. I hope I do your friendship justice.

Wyddershyns
Unexpected Life Stories

In this collection of reminiscences and short stories, Polly J. Fry creates whole worlds in bite-sized chunks. Each selection of tales is punctuated by a memoir from Fry's life, paying tribute to the people who shared the good times and guided her – unknowingly – through difficult times.

The stories range from the everyday adventures of the wonderfully engaging Mrs Khan through to science fiction, mystery and romance. Fry even reimagines some of Shakespeare's characters, who decide to swop plays, the consequences leading to a myriad twists and turns,

There's something here for everyone.

Mrs Khan and the W.I. Bucket List

The indomitable Mrs Khan has really started something. Spurred on by her mastery of the harp in later life, the women of the Stackton-on-Sea W.I. are determined to help each other achieve their dreams. With this is mind, they create the Bucket List.

There's **Val**, adapting to being a first-time newlywed in retirement years

Dorothy, the chocolatier set on a visit to a cocoa bean plantation

Lally, sorting out the future for herself and her little daughter, Chelsea

and

Helena, going for a career on the stage.

And who is The Wizard?

Join them and find out how they get on

Printed in Great Britain
by Amazon